Feels like Heaven

a novel

VANESSA MILLER

WHITAKER
HOUSE

FEELS LIKE HEAVEN
My Soul to Keep ~ Book One

Vanessa Miller
www.vanessamiller.com

ISBN: 978-1-62911-008-0
eBook ISBN: 978-1-62911-032-5
Printed in the United States of America
© 2014 by Vanessa Miller

Whitaker House
1030 Hunt Valley Circle
New Kensington, PA 15068
www.whitakerhouse.com

Library of Congress Cataloging-in-Publication Data

Miller, Vanessa.

Feels like Heaven / by Vanessa Miller.

pages cm.—(My soul to keep ; book 1)

ISBN 978-1-62911-008-0 (pbk.)—ISBN 978-1-62911-032-5 (eBook) 1. Fathers and sons—Fiction. 2. Parent and adult child—Fiction. 3. Illegitimate children—Family relationships—Fiction. 4. Families—Fiction. I. Title.

PS3613.I5623F44 2014

813'.6—dc23

2014010094

1 2 3 4 5 6 7 8 9 10 11 ⦿ 20 19 18 17 16 15 14

DEDICATION

To my daughter, Erin Miller...for love that feels like heaven. It's in your future, so keep holding on to God's hand as He leads you to it.

ACKNOWLEDGMENTS

I have written a lot of books and have never run out of people to thank for their love and support. It is true that no man is an island unto himself; we all need someone if we are ever to see our dreams come to life. So, I would first like to thank Bob Whitaker Jr. and Christine Whitaker for seeing the potential in my writing and giving my books a place to call home. I couldn't have found a nicer editor to work with than Courtney Hartzel, so I want to thank her for her patience and all the work she puts in to my projects in order to create the masterpieces that go out to my readers. Each person I have worked with at Whitaker House, from the marketing department to the publicity department, has been wonderful to work with, so I must give a heartfelt thank-you to everyone at Whitaker House.

My wonderful agent, Natasha Kern, has always been in my corner, and I would like to thank her for working out the deal for the series My Soul to Keep.

No acknowledgments page would be complete without an acknowledgment of my faithful readers. Many of you have stuck with me throughout the years and purchased every book that I have written, and your kindness toward me has not gone unnoticed. I appreciate each and every one of you, and I would like to take this opportunity to say thanks. Don't forget to e-mail me and let me know what you think of *Feels like Heaven!*

—*Vanessa Miller*

PROLOGUE

*A*ttorney Solomon Harris put on his Dolce & Gabbana shades and stepped outside the courthouse with Dwight Blackshear, fitness instructor to the stars. The media was waiting to pounce. No one had expected Dwight to walk out of the courthouse a free man—not when he'd been accused of murdering a Hollywood legend in her own home. But Solomon had been convinced of his client's innocence from the very beginning and had fought a good fight in order to secure his acquittal. "Be cool as the reporters approach," Solomon whispered in his client's ear as the media circus surrounded them. "Don't say anything. Let me do the talking."

"Mr. Blackshear, how do you feel after getting away with murder?" one reporter asked, holding a microphone in Dwight's face.

"No comment," Solomon said, pushing the mic aside.

"Did the jury get it right?" another journalist asked.

"What's your next move, Dwight? Do you think anyone will ever let you into their home again to train them?"

On and on, the questions kept coming. But Solomon was feeling pretty good about his chances of getting inside the waiting car without his client opening his big mouth and ruining any chances of rebuilding a career in the City of Angels. But then came the question that Dwight's ego couldn't let slide—the question that would send months of Solomon's hard work up in smoke.

"What happened, Dwight? Did Victoria Price want to trade you in for a younger instructor?"

Dwight grabbed the reporter by the throat as he declared, "I'm the best at what I do. I'm fifty-three and in the best shape of my life. No one could ever replace me."

Solomon pried Dwight's hands off the reporter and rushed him to the car. The instant the doors closed and his driver sped away from the courthouse, Solomon laid into Dwight. "You want to tell me what that was all about?"

Dwight shrugged. "He insulted me. I'm no washed-up has-been. I helped build this town."

"Those reporters and their viewers believe that Victoria Price helped build this town, with all of the movies she starred in. And none of them will appreciate the man accused with her murder being acquitted and, on the same day, trying to strangle someone before making it past the courthouse steps."

"I don't care what they think," Dwight groused. "Victoria deserved everything she got. That hag went around telling everyone who'd listen that I was responsible for her ten-pound weight gain."

Solomon leaned back in his seat, and as his eyes swept across Dwight, he realized for the first time that he was staring at a killer. When Dwight had first come to his office, he'd told Solomon that he would swear on a stack of Bibles, if necessary, to convince the jury that he hadn't strangled Victoria Price. He'd told Solomon that he adored Victoria and that she had been one of the first people to hire him as a personal trainer. But now that he had been acquitted, Dwight didn't have a problem expressing his true feelings about the late actress.

"Instead of training actors, you should have been one yourself," Solomon told him. "You really had me fooled, and that's not easy to do."

"I came to this town to become an actor, but fitness ended up being my ticket to stardom," Dwight said. "That's why I couldn't let Victoria ruin my reputation. You understand, don't you?"

Oh, he understood alright. He had been duped by a sociopath. Dwight couldn't make himself care about another human being other than himself if he wanted to, but he sure could pretend to care. Solomon had always prided himself on his ability to read people—to know when he was being lied to—but he'd missed this one.

"Don't look so disheartened, Solomon," Dwight told him. "You did a bang-up job in the courtroom. If I ever need help like this again, I'll be sure to call on you."

When they pulled up to Dwight's house, Dwight opened the door, but Solomon grabbed his arm before he could step outside. "You might not want to go on a killing spree, because I quit. I will not represent you again."

Pulling his arm away, Dwight laughed as he got out of the car.

Solomon slammed the door shut. "My office," he told his driver.

During the drive, Solomon leaned back in his seat and did a mental analysis of how he had come to represent a killer—something he had always said he would never do. He was well aware that as a defense attorney, he was within his legal rights to represent the guilty as well as the innocent. But he never liked dealing with people who threw rocks and then hid their hands.

During his years of law school, Solomon had asked God to bless his mind and anoint him as an advocate for his clients. He had promised in return that he would not aid the guilty to get away with crimes against humanity but would use the wisdom with which God endowed him only to help the unjustly accused.

Too bad the law firm of People, Smith, and Harding didn't care about the bargain Solomon had made with God.

As he got out of the car and headed into his office, Solomon was left to wonder what this would mean for his career with the firm. Would God still bless his mind so that he could help the innocent? Or had he burned his own house down by his inability to discern evil when it looked him in the face?

"Good morning, Mr. Harris," his secretary greeted him, then handed him a few slips of paper. "Here are your messages. And your mother is waiting for you in your office."

His mother rarely visited him at the office. She always told him how proud she was of the important work he was doing, and said that she wouldn't dream of disturbing him during the day over trivial matters that could be discussed later in the evening. So, Solomon knew that something was troubling her.

When he opened his office door, he saw the nervous look in her eyes. "What's wrong?" he asked, closing the door behind him.

She patted the seat next to her. "Come sit with your mother."

Solomon joined her on the black leather sofa, but he didn't get comfortable. He couldn't, with the way she was looking at him. "Tell me."

His mother took a deep breath and put her hand over his. "It's your father."

Solomon furrowed his brow. "My *who?*"

"Don't play coy with me. You know you have a father...and he's dying."

CHAPTER 1

Sitting in the hospital room while his half sisters and their mother fussed over the great senior pastor of the Worship Center of God, Solomon was out of his element. He felt like a lurker and didn't know how much longer he could continue witnessing this spectacle from the back of the room. David Davison's wife, Alma, and their daughters fretted over him as if he was something precious and necessary.

The door opened, and Solomon's half brother, Adam, rushed in. Solomon recognized him from the family portrait he'd seen on the church Web site. Solomon had never been formally introduced to anyone in this room...never been invited to dinner or allowed to spend holidays or summer vacations with this family. That was why he was truly puzzled as to the reason why he'd been summoned to his father's bedside. David Davison had never wanted anything to do with him before.

"I brought some documents for you to sign, Dad," Adam said. He placed a stack of papers on the tray in front of his father and handed him a pen.

"Church business must go on, huh, Son? Even when I'm in the hospital fighting for my life."

Hearing this man call Adam "Son" was more than Solomon could take. He'd thought he'd gotten over his anger about having a father who sent checks to him and his mother but admonished them to keep their distance. So much distance that his mother had left North Carolina when Solomon was still in diapers and moved them back to California, where she had a few family members.

As David signed the papers, one of the sisters asked Adam how things were going at the church.

"Everything is fine," Adam assured her. "The members are excited for Dad's return, but they are still being fed the Word of God while he's here in the hospital."

"Thank you for everything you're doing, Son. God's work must go on."

Enough already. Solomon got up and headed for the door without saying anything to anyone. None of them had spoken two words to him, anyway.

"Wait a minute, Solomon. Don't leave," David said. "I need to introduce you to your family."

Solomon stopped and turned around. He wanted to tell him that the only family he'd ever known—his mother—was at home in California. But he was curious as to how the old man would explain himself to his children, so he held his tongue and waited.

David handed the papers back to Adam and then clasped hands with his wife, as if they were joining forces. He looked at her with so much love in his eyes that Solomon had to wonder why he cheated on a woman he seemed to love so much. Alma nodded at David, and he turned to face his children, who eyed him curiously.

"Adam, Tamara, and Leah, I was trying to wait for Larissa, but I can't put this off any longer." He swallowed hard, then nodded toward Solomon. "I want to introduce all of you to your brother. His name is Solomon Harris."

The moment the words were out of his mouth, the room erupted with shouts and confusion, to the point that a nurse came in and asked everyone to settle down.

Tamara glared at Solomon. "How old are you?"

"Thirty-two," he answered quickly, then waited for them to put it all together.

Adam turned to his father. "I'm thirty-three, Dad. Are you telling me that you had another son while married to Mama before I was even out of diapers?"

David lowered his head. "I did, Son. You are correct."

To Solomon, David Davison looked like a man who was truly ashamed of his actions. But that didn't comfort Solomon. It made him feel as if he should be ashamed to be alive. Thanks to the love and guidance of Sheila Harris, Solomon had never been ashamed of who he was…until now. He didn't need this. Shaking his head, he left the room of his so-called father and strode down the hall. He wanted no part in the family drama that was playing out in that hospital room right now.

As he rounded the corner, his mind was so set on getting out of there as fast as he could that he didn't notice the woman headed his way until he had bumped into her and watched her fall to the ground. "I'm so sorry," he said, reaching down to pull her up to her feet again.

"What's the hurry?" She grabbed hold of his arm and eyed him with confusion.

Solomon almost dropped her on the floor again, so startled he was by her beauty—especially her eyes, a gorgeous light gray with a hint of brown. Her features were movie-star quality, and Solomon had seen his share of movie stars. But he couldn't think of a single star whose presence he would have rather been in at this very moment. "Sorry again. I wasn't paying attention." He released her. "Are you okay?"

Dusting off the back of her pants, she told him, "I'll live. I just had no idea that hospitals were so dangerous."

"Trust me, you don't want to hang around here. Hospitals are the worst places for anyone, sick or well."

"And how would you know that? Are you a doctor?"

"I'm a lawyer, and the firm I work for sues doctors and hospitals on the regular." Solomon shook his head. "Too many mistakes. Makes you wonder if any of the 'medical professionals' were paying attention in class."

"Is that right?" The woman folded her arms across her chest.

"I could tell you stories." Solomon took a business card out of his pocket and handed it to her. "I'm in a hurry right now, but I'd love to take you to dinner this evening. We can trade stories if you make it out of this place alive." He was giving her the grin that showed off his dimples, and he hoped she saw them. Women liked his dimples.

Glancing at his card, she said, "Thanks for the offer, Mr. Harris, but I don't think so."

His face fell, but then he smiled at her again. Women were always telling him how infectious his smile was. Maybe she'd missed it on the first go-round. "I know I knocked you down and all, and you might be holding that against me, but I'm really a nice guy. Honest."

Before she could respond, Alma Davison rounded the corner. "Thank God you're here, Dr. Wilkinson," she said to the woman. "I think he needs you now."

"You're a doctor?" Solomon wished he could just put his foot in his mouth and shut up already. He'd messed up with this beautiful woman, all because he'd insulted her profession. But how could he have known she was a doctor? She wasn't wearing one of those white coats most doctors paraded around in.

Dr. Wilkinson walked off without answering. Then Alma turned to Solomon. "I came looking for you."

"And why is that?" All of the good-natured humor Solomon had tried to display moments ago was gone.

"Your father needs you with him. He's not well, and if you leave now, I just don't know what might happen."

"Don't try to guilt-trip me." Solomon pointed down the hall toward his father's room. "Where was he when I needed him? All those years of growing up without a father in my life...he certainly didn't care about that."

"He cared, Solomon." She looked away and then back at him. "If anyone is to blame for the absence of a father in your life, it's me. David sent money to your mother every month and paid everything that scholarships didn't cover for your schooling, but I refused to let him have a relationship with you." She bit her lip. "I see how much I hurt him—and you—because of my bitterness. But I don't want my husband to die. And right now, I truly believe that you're our best hope of getting him out of this hospital." Tears were running down her face as she continued. "I know I have no right to ask you for anything, but please...don't leave. Please stay and talk to him."

"Your kids don't want me here. They knew nothing about me until today."

"I know. But if you give them a chance, I think you all will become great friends."

Solomon scoffed. "I already have enough friends."

Alma looked distressed. "Blame me, Solomon. It's my fault that you don't know your family. But don't punish David. Please don't walk out on him."

"How is everything your fault when he's the one who slept with my mother?" Solomon saw Alma flinch at his words, but he was so angry, he didn't care. He didn't even care about the people passing by. As a matter of fact, he wished he could go down to his wonderful father's church and tell the entire congregation what the good pastor had been up to all these years.

Alma glanced up and down the hall and then whispered, "The sleeping around was David's fault. But that happened a long time ago, and I'm tired of making you and him pay for a thirty-year-old indiscretion. So, you can be mad at me all you want, but your father wants to see you. And I hope you won't deny him this request."

Solomon had never heard those words before. Not once in his entire life had anyone come to him and said, "Your father wants to see you." A part of him wanted to ask her to say it again. But he reminded himself that he was a full-grown man and was well past the time when he needed to come running when his father called.

"Please," Alma begged.

If her words were to be believed, this woman had denied him a father for over thirty years, and now she was pleading with him to do her a favor. Solomon could have given her a dose of her own medicine, but he wasn't that cruel. "Let me make a call, and then I'll come back to see what he has to say."

She patted his shoulder. "Thank you."

Solomon stepped outside to get better reception on his cell phone. He leaned against the building and called his mother. She answered on the first ring.

"What's going on? Are you okay?" she asked before he could get a word out of his mouth.

"I don't know about these people." If he had been seven years old on a visit to his father's house, he would have been saying something like, "I want to come back home." But he wasn't seven, and he didn't have to ask for permission to leave if that was what he wanted to do. Still, Solomon hated disappointing his mother. She'd already experienced enough let-downs to last a lifetime.

"They're not that bad," she insisted. "You just have to give them a chance."

"Mom, I don't believe you sometimes. These people ran you out of town, and you're defending them."

"Nobody ran me out of town, boy. I left because I needed a do-over… for you and for me. I knew that what I did wasn't right, and I didn't want you living with the consequences of my actions every day of your life."

"News flash, Mom: I lived with those consequences every day I woke up without a father in the house."

"I'm sorry, Solomon." She sighed. "I was young and stupid back then. I hadn't even bothered to take two seconds to consider what the next day would bring. But, as God is my witness, I have repented of my actions and spent a long time praying that your life would be blessed in spite of the circumstances of your birth."

He could hear the quaver in her voice. The last thing he wanted to do was to make his mother cry. "You did a good job raising me, Mom," he assured her. "I wouldn't be where I am now if it wasn't for you."

After a moment, she cleared her throat, then continued. "I know you don't want to hear this, but your father had a lot to do with where you are now, too. If he hadn't kept up his end of the bargain, we wouldn't have been able to live in a decent neighborhood, and Lord only knows what would have happened to you if one of those gangs had gotten ahold of you. And we sure wouldn't have been able to afford your college, even with the partial scholarship you received."

"He didn't do any more than he had to," Solomon muttered.

"No, Solomon, that's not true. I have friends who have never seen a dime of child support from the deadbeats they had children by."

"So, what am I supposed to do? Thank him for sending those checks, even though he never bothered to show up or call on birthdays or Christmases or that time I broke my arm?"

His mother sighed again. "You're a grown man, so I can't tell you what to do anymore. But you were raised in the church, and I know that you have the ability to forgive and move on—if not for your father's sake then for your own."

Solomon rolled his eyes. "I'll call you again in a little while, Mom. I need to get back in there." Then he made his way up to the third floor, to his father's room. He figured he'd come all this way, he might as well hear the man out. He had no idea what his father would say to make up for all these years, but Solomon knew one thing for sure: He wasn't about to offer up any of that forgiveness his mother had talked about. Not today.

CHAPTER 2

"What's with all the sad faces?" Larissa Wilkinson asked as she walked into the hospital room of her godfather, Uncle David. She knew that his prognosis hadn't been good, but the Davisons were people of faith. And even though she was a doctor and loved the study of medicine, Larissa wanted to believe that there was something out there bigger than science. Her godfather preached about it every Sunday, but it didn't seem as if anyone in this room had caught on to any of his messages. "Do I have any water-walkers in here? Uncle David is going to pull through just fine, so stop with all the frowning."

"We know that Daddy is going to walk out of this hospital," Tamara told her. "We're not worried about that."

"Then what's the problem?"

Aunt Alma came back into the room and told her husband, "He's going to make a call, but he'll be back in a few minutes."

Uncle David sighed in relief. "Thank God."

"How can you thank God for an illegitimate son?" Leah asked. "What you did wasn't right, Daddy."

"Have I missed something?" Larissa looked around the room, hoping that someone would fill her in.

"Your uncle has another son," Alma told her.

Larissa's hand went to her mouth, but not before a gasp escaped. As long as she'd been a part of the Davisons' lives, all she'd ever known was how happy her aunt and uncle were. She never would have suspected something like this. Her godfather was a good, God-fearing man. He couldn't have done what he was being accused of doing. Larissa would never believe it unless she heard it straight from her godfather's mouth. "Why would Aunt Alma say something like that? Tell her it's not true, Uncle David. Tell her."

He sighed. "It's true, hon. Your aunt and I struggled for many years after my indiscretion. But I'm thankful that she found it in her heart to forgive me." Uncle David joined hands with Aunt Alma.

Tamara shook her head. "I don't understand this at all. How could you forgive Daddy after what he did to you?"

"And Daddy, you're a preacher," Leah put in. "How could you continue standing behind that pulpit knowing what you did to our family? I'm sorry, but I find all of this so very hypocritical." She glanced around the room. "Am I the only one who feels this way?"

"First of all," Aunt Alma began, "your daddy wasn't a preacher when this happened. We had been married all of two years, and to tell you the truth, we didn't really like each other all that much. I moved back home with my mother, and your daddy found himself a girlfriend. My mother suggested marriage counseling, and thankfully, the counselor we picked was a born-again Christian. David gave his life to the Lord and then told me everything he had been doing. He begged me to forgive him. I didn't want to at first, because I was hurt by his actions. But I'm so glad I did. Because our life together since then has been more than I ever could have dreamed of.

"But I kept him from his son, because the only thing I couldn't forgive was the fact that he'd had another child. The only way I could love him again was to pretend that the child—his child—didn't exist." Aunt Alma lowered her head. "So, don't blame your father for your not knowing that you had a brother. He wanted to tell you a long time ago. It was only your father's love for me that kept him from revealing any of this to all of you."

Adam started pacing the room. "Okay, what's done is done. But why bring him here now? You can't mean to introduce him to the congregation as your long-lost son. Imagine how many members will leave the church! It's unthinkable, Dad. You can't do it."

Uncle David gave a sad smile. "That's just what I plan to do, Son. But first I'll have to get out of this bed so I can return to church."

"There's no need for you to rush back," Adam said. "I've got things covered."

"Even if Daddy doesn't go back to the church right away, we still have a problem," Leah interjected. "We just can't take Solomon to church with us and start introducing him to people as our brother. We need a plan." She handled public relations at the church, and she probably viewed this as the biggest potential crisis she had ever needed to contain.

"I don't see what the big deal is," Larissa said. "This all happened before Uncle David became a pastor, and he and Aunt Alma were separated at the time. Just tell the church the truth, and let that be that." When the bomb was first dropped, Larissa had been horrified and had desperately wanted her uncle to deny every word. But now that the story had been explained, she was no longer devastated. She knew that even people who loved each other deeply often went through

rough patches, but, as they said, all's well that ends well. And Larissa believed with every fiber of her being that things would always end well for her aunt and uncle.

Tamara rolled her eyes and wrapped her arms around her front. "Of course, you wouldn't view this as a problem," she told Larissa. "You're used to having parents who bring shame to their family. But this is all new to me. So, y'all are going to have to give me a minute."

"Tamara, you watch your mouth," Aunt Alma admonished her daughter. "You will not disparage Larissa's mother in my presence."

Tamara looked away. "Sorry. I was just trying to say that revealing this information is going to be embarrassing to us, your children. So, I would like a little consideration shown for how I'm going to feel once everyone knows that my father had a secret life and a secret child that no one knew about."

"Baby girl, I understand your frustration, but it's way past time," Uncle David said as he squeezed Aunt Alma's hand. "I owe Solomon much more than I've given to him. I don't even know if he'll let me be a part of his life, but I want that very much, and I'll need all of you to help me make that happen."

Solomon slowly opened the door to his father's hospital room and peeked in. "Am I interrupting something?"

"Of course not," David said, waving him inside. "Come over here, Solomon. It's time for you to take your rightful place in this family."

His mom had asked him to forgive, but hearing those words come out of his father's mouth made that concept a lot harder for Solomon. "I don't know what's going on in here, but I didn't fly all the way to Charlotte to be inducted into your perfect little family. I just want to know why you summoned me here after all these years. Then we can all go back to living our lives."

David pointed to the empty chair next to his bed. "Have a seat, Solomon. I want to discuss my will with my children."

"Now, Dad, you've gone too far," Adam protested. "You want us to accept the fact that you had another child while you were married to Mama. Okay. But we don't know anything about him." He gave Solomon a suspicious glance. "And I certainly don't think he needs to be involved in any discussions about your will."

Solomon wasn't concerned about the reading of any will. What disturbed him was that the beautiful doctor he'd almost run over in the hallway was still in the room. She was seated with the family, as if her reason for being there was personal rather than professional. Solomon figured he wouldn't be getting that date, no matter how much he begged. He pointed at the woman and asked David, "Is she your daughter? How many extra kids on the side do you have?"

Laughing, David extended a hand toward the doctor. She stood and went to him, grasping his hand. "Larissa is my goddaughter. We raised her from the time she was ten years old." He nodded to his wife. "She's Alma's niece."

Solomon was getting a headache. He would rather do just about anything else than be here right now. Turning to Alma, he asked, "If she's family, then why did you call her 'Dr. Wilkinson'?"

"Larissa just finished her residency and passed her boards." Alma shrugged her shoulders. "I like calling her 'doctor.' She's the first one in our family."

"And I can assure you that I did pay attention in class," Larissa told Solomon with a smirk on her face.

"I didn't mean any harm. If I had known you were a doctor, I never would have said those things." Solomon was sweating. He had offended this beautiful woman and had probably ruined his chances of getting to know her.

Waving a hand in the air, Larissa said, "Don't worry about it. Since you're family, I guess I have to forgive you."

"You're her niece," Solomon quickly said, pointing at Alma. "So you and I are definitely not related. Don't get it twisted."

"If you don't want to be my family, fine—don't consider me family. I'm not begging anyone to let me in. I had enough of that from my cousins when I was a kid." She nodded, indicating David's legitimate children.

"Yeah, sure, life was so hard for you with private school, vacations around the world, and expensive education paid for by my father," Leah sassed. "My heart just bleeds for you."

"I wasn't talking to you, Leah, so butt out." Turning back to Solomon, Larissa said, "Having cousins is way overrated."

"I am not your cousin!" Solomon practically yelled. He saw the irritation on her face and figured it had something to do with the way she'd been treated by his half siblings. He knew the feeling, because they hadn't been all warm and fussy with him, either. But he wasn't interested in being kissing cousins, so Larissa was just going to have to get over any thought of the two of them being related.

"Okay, you all, can we get back to the reason I asked everyone here this morning?" David asked.

The room fell silent.

"All of you will be splitting the twenty million I have earned during my lifetime."

"Splitting how?" Adam wanted to know.

"David and I have discussed this at length," Alma said. "Our home is paid off, and if anything happened to him, I would continue receiving the royalties from his books and movies. I would also have the money in our retirement plan, but we want to split whatever is in the bank account with our children, and that includes Solomon and Larissa."

"That's outrageous!" Leah exclaimed. "Have you lost your minds?" Her eyes shot daggers at Solomon and Larissa.

"We think it's more than fair," Alma said. "None of you worked for this money, so you can't tell us how to divide it up."

"Whatever," Tamara groused.

"Before you three get upset about this, you need to understand that the money I've earned is in jeopardy," David explained. "If we don't all band together, you might not get anything." He swallowed hard, then lifted his head so Alma could fluff the pillow behind him.

"What are you talking about?" Adam asked.

"You all have enough to deal with, just knowing that I'm sick, but your mother and I don't want to hide anything else. We want to treat you like the grown-ups you are and tell you what's going on."

Adam stood at the foot of the bed, looking as if he was steeling himself for the other shoe that was about to drop. "Just tell us, Daddy."

"Alright." David nodded. "I am currently being sued and stand a chance of losing every dime of your inheritance." He then proceeded to tell them about the woman who was threatening to sue him.

When he was finished, Solomon said, "So let me get this straight: A woman is suing you for messing around with her underage daughter, and you want us all to believe that you didn't do it."

"I didn't do it, Son."

"Don't call me that." Solomon flared his nostrils as he swiveled his head, looking from one family member to the next. "Is anybody else buying this?"

Larissa raised her hand. "I believe him."

"And so do I," Alma declared.

"How can you be so confident, Mama?" Leah asked. "I mean, we have evidence right in this room that says Daddy does cheat."

Alma smiled at her husband. "And I have almost thirty years of evidence that tells me I am married to a man who loves God and his wife so much that he doesn't desire to do anything that would harm either relationship."

"You can have faith in pimping preachers if you want, but all I ask is that you all leave me out of it." Solomon was about ready to walk out of this room again and get back to California.

"That's my father you're talking about," Tamara spat, her voice dripping venom. "He may have made a mistake by having you, but he's a good man. And you don't get to come in here and talk about him like that."

Solomon couldn't believe how these people were defending their philandering father. Why had Solomon wasted his time flying all the way here? The man hadn't changed. He was still the same old cheat who'd stepped out on his wife on the regular. "You all can believe whatever you want to. I'm out of here."

"Wait!" David said. "You can't leave. I want you to represent me."

Solomon swung around, eyes bulging out of his head. "Are you nuts? You don't bother to show up for one birthday or Christmas, and then you call me down here when you finally get what's coming to you, and ask me"—Solomon jabbed a finger at his chest—"to represent you?"

David grinned mischievously as he said, "I did pay for your education. I figure the least you could do is help your old man out of a jam."

"I don't represent guilty people. I went into law to help the innocent."

"He is innocent," Larissa snapped.

"That's what they all say." Solomon wasn't backing down. He wasn't interested in having another Dwight Blackshear on his hands.

"Why don't you go to dinner with Larissa?" David suggested. "If you two can sit down and discuss this, I think she will be able to convince you of my innocence."

Solomon wasn't so sure about that. But he'd wanted to take Larissa out from the moment he'd first looked into those gorgeous eyes of hers. He wasn't about to pass up this opportunity, even if it meant having to talk about his absentee father.

CHAPTER 3

"I'm telling you right now, Larissa, if you go out with him, I will never speak to you again," Leah declared.

Leah had always been bitter and unyielding. Larissa had never been able to forge a friendship with her, or with Tamara or Adam, because she'd always felt that they were taking something that should have been hers.

"What difference does that make?" Larissa retorted. "You barely speak to me as it is."

"You and I have always been close, Larissa," said Tamara. "And I'm telling you that I don't like this, either. How can Daddy just force Solomon on us simply because he made a mistake?"

"I know this doesn't seem fair, but Uncle David needs Solomon's help. If he wants me to talk with him about what I know, I don't see the harm in that." Larissa put her hands on her hips and stared at her cousins with a look of defiance.

"Daddy can get another lawyer," Leah barked. "He doesn't need Solomon for this upcoming case. He just wants him here to rub our noses in the fact that he has another child."

"I don't think he wants to rub your nose in anything," Larissa said. "I think he just wants his son to represent him. Shouldn't that be enough explanation for us?"

"Daddy probably did it," Leah said.

Tamara gasped. "How can you say such a thing? Daddy has never lied to us, and if he says he didn't do this thing, then I believe him."

"Be naive if you want to," Leah said, "but he lied to us about Solomon, not telling us anything for all these years. I'm not going to believe what he says without proof of his innocence."

"I still believe him," Larissa declared. "And I'll move heaven and earth to help him prove his innocence. If that means going to dinner with Solomon Harris, then that's what I'm going to do. Now, if you ladies will excuse me, I have a date to get ready for."

***

Solomon tried to act like having dinner with a beautiful gray-eyed woman was something he did at least once a week. Holding the menu in front of his face and pretending to study it when he knew good and well that this was going to be a steak-and-potatoes night, Solomon tried to come up with something witty to say to Larissa. Something that would get her laughing and smiling at him.

But he was so nervous that he managed to botch simple dinner conversation. After the server had taken their orders and Larissa had asked for not just lobster but steak, too, Solomon said, "Dang, girl, you can eat. Good thing Daddy Warbucks is paying for this meal."

"If you must know, I haven't eaten all day," she replied. "And I really don't appreciate you calling Uncle David 'Daddy Warbucks.' It doesn't sound right when you speak of a man of God like that."

"What'd I say wrong?" He frowned. "I'm simply acknowledging that God has opened a window in heaven and poured out a blessing that Pastor Davison doesn't have room enough to receive."

"That's not what you meant at all."

"That's exactly what I meant. But I also can see that Pastor Davison has taken it upon himself to add a few women to his list of blessings. And I don't think God told him to do that at all."

"You're wrong about Uncle David."

"I guess that's why you agreed to have dinner with me—to explain why I'm wrong," Solomon said. "So, I'm all ears. I'm ready to listen."

When their food arrived, Larissa said grace, then sliced into her medium-well rib eye. She forked a piece into her mouth and closed her eyes as she chewed. "Mm-mm-mm, this steak is too good. I can't ruin my eating experience by talking to a doubting Thomas. We can discuss Uncle David when I'm done."

Solomon bit into his own steak and understood exactly why Larissa would rather eat than spar with him. He didn't feel much like arguing his point at that moment, either. "My goodness, you're right. That cow must've lived a good life."

In spite of trying to hold it in, Larissa laughed. "You are goofy." She wiped her mouth with her napkin. "Here's the deal. Uncle David is being set up." Before Solomon could respond, she lifted a hand. "How do I know? Because I volunteer at the church."

"I'm sure the church has hundreds of volunteers, but not one of them could tell us what happened behind closed doors," Solomon remarked.

Larissa shook her head. "While I was in residency, I was trying to determine if I had made the right choice of profession. You see, I had always thought I would go into psychology. Uncle David offered me a chance to do hands-on work at the church. So, what I'm trying to tell you is that I was present for every counseling session Winter had with him."

Solomon put his fork down and wiped his mouth. "If you were at each session, why is the mother now claiming that the good pastor touched her child?"

"Like I said, he's being set up. That's the only explanation. The whole situation seemed strange to me from the very beginning." Larissa pushed her plate away and continued, "Summer Jones complained about her child's disobedience and begged Uncle David to counsel her, but then the mother would always make up some excuse as to why she couldn't attend the sessions with the child she claimed to want to help so badly."

As much as it pained Solomon to admit it, that didn't sound right. "What excuses did the mother come up with?"

"It was always something about work. We finally told her that if she couldn't make time for the counseling sessions, we would not schedule another appointment for her daughter. That was about six months ago."

"And were they still attending the church?"

Larissa took a moment to think about that. She tilted her head to the side and looked off into space as if trying to jog her memory. When she turned back to Solomon, she said, "I hadn't thought much of it, but no, I haven't seen them around the church since we ended the counseling sessions. She was probably just mad that we weren't babysitting her daughter anymore and went to find another pastor who would watch her kid while she worked."

"But if she had been a member at your church, I really can't see them leaving just because you asked her to attend the counseling sessions."

"People are strange these days. Sometimes it seems you can't tell a blood-bought Christian from a rank sinner." Larissa shook her head.

"Your eyes are too beautiful to hold so much sadness," Solomon told her. "What's on your mind?"

"Oh, nothing." She forced a smile. "I just don't understand how someone could slander a man of God like that. It's as if people have no fear of God these days."

"I'm sorry that it pains you so much," he said, meaning it. "I guess I'm just jaded. In my line of work, I deal with people who wouldn't fear God unless He came down from heaven and knocked them in the head."

Larissa laughed. "You're pretty funny, Solomon. Just like your dad. And you know what?"

"What?"

"You look like him, too."

Solomon quickly changed the subject. "I'm really enjoying this dinner...the food and the company. It's too bad I have to head back to California in the morning, because I'd really like to see you again."

Larissa had been leaning back in her chair, but she shot forward and grabbed hold of Solomon's arm. "You can't leave. Uncle David needs you. If you go home now, he might have another heart attack."

"I'm sure he can find someone else to represent him. He's been recovering for more than a week without my presence. I doubt if he needs me to survive."

"Aunt Alma has been handling things for him. He tells her what he wants, and she has been moving heaven and earth to make it happen."

"She's too good for him, if you ask me."

"Good thing no one asked you." Larissa stood. "I'm ready to go. I'll be waiting for you outside."

Was it something I said? Solomon was left alone at the table, again wondering how he had managed to put his foot in it again. He paid the bill and then went outside to make his apologies.

⌖

Wearing out the concrete as she waited on Solomon to come out of the restaurant, Larissa was caught between two conflicting thoughts: *He's dreamy gorgeous* and *He's spiteful and mean.* He'd made her laugh a few times, and she'd let down her guard. She'd felt comfortable with him and believed that she would be able to talk him over to their side. But that last crack had let her know that she was just wasting her time.

She had worked herself up so bad as she paced back and forth that when Solomon met up with her, she wagged her finger in his face and said, "You've got a lot of nerve, refusing to help your own father, who paid your college tuition and more."

Solomon raised his eyebrows. "I came out here to apologize to you for being rude, but with the way you're wagging that finger, I'd say you owe me an apology." He walked past her and flung back over his shoulder, "Come on. That is, unless you've decided to walk home."

Larissa might be upset with Solomon, but she wasn't crazy. She rushed to follow him to the car, all the while wishing she had driven herself. "You're a real charmer, you know that?" she said as she climbed into the car and fastened her seat belt.

Solomon slammed his door and put the key in the ignition, but instead of backing out of the parking spot, he pointed his finger in Larissa's face and said, "You know something? You're the one who has a lot of nerve passing judgment on me."

"I wasn't judging you."

"Oh, you were judging me, and you have no right. They took you in. You lived with them, and he took care of you just like you were his own child. Meanwhile, I never even saw his face. Until you know how it feels to pray night after night for your father to bless you with his presence, you have no right to judge me." He didn't say another word to her as he pulled out of the parking lot and drove the streets of Charlotte.

Larissa wanted to tell him that she knew exactly how it felt. Since she was ten years old, she had been praying that her father would come back home and make everything right again. But he never did, and she'd stayed with her aunt and uncle until she went off to college because her mom was too busy being crazy to take care of the child she'd brought into the world.

"I do know how you feel," she said softly. "Even though my aunt and uncle were wonderful surrogates, I still longed for my own father." Sighing deeply, she added, "I'm sorry for what I said. You do have a right to be angry."

He glanced over at her, then quickly turned back to face the road. "Thanks for saying that."

"And I'm sorry that Aunt Alma put such a condition on her love. Believe it or not, they are good people."

"I believe they were good to you. But I can't personally vouch for their goodness."

"Well, you turned out alright, even without Uncle David being there."

Solomon nodded. "I have a strong mother. She wasn't putting up with my foolishness. When I was growing up, there was no such thing as too sick to go to school or too tired to do homework."

"Sounds like your mother knew how to keep you in line."

"Oh, she knew how, alright. And she believed the Bible a little too literally when it said, 'Spare the rod, spoil the child.'"

Laughing, Larissa told him, "Aunt Alma was that way, too. Uncle David is a big old softy, but Auntie don't play."

"You talk like you had it rough. But you don't know rough until you've lived under Sheila Harris's roof. That woman terrorized me so much with that baseball bat of hers that I couldn't wait to get out of that house."

"She had a baseball bat?"

"Yeah, and she wasn't afraid to use it, either. At least, that's what she told me anytime she thought I was 'smelling myself,' as she called it." Solomon turned onto Larissa's street. "As I grew up, I realized that it would have killed my mom to have to hit me with that bat, but she knew she was raising a boy and had to be firm with me."

"Your mom was smart. She knew what it took to keep you on the straight and narrow."

"I strayed off that path a few times," Solomon confessed as he pulled into her driveway and parked the car, "but in the end, I just didn't like to see that disappointed look on her face. I would always pray for the strength to do the right thing so I could make my mama proud."

"I'm sure she's proud. You finished law school, didn't you?"

Solomon nodded.

"And you're working for a big law firm. What's not to be proud of?"

Solomon twisted his lips. "A law firm that keeps assigning me dud clients."

"Do me a favor," Larissa said as she opened the car door. "Think about what I told you, and if you come to the conclusion that there is even a slim chance that Uncle David might be innocent, then take his case, okay?" When Solomon hesitated, she added, "He's being set up. I'm sure of it. And he really needs your help."

Solomon looked her in the eye. "I'll think it over if you agree to have dinner with me again."

Larissa smiled. She'd had such a good time talking with Solomon on the drive home that she wouldn't mind seeing him again. Only one problem. "You do know that I'm your cousin, right?"

"For the last time, we are not related!" Solomon reached over and took her face in his hands. "My father is your uncle through marriage, so doing this is totally allowed." He put his mouth on hers and gave her a soft, gentle kiss.

Larissa's head began to swim. She leaned away from him, opened the door wider, and stepped out of the car. Before shutting the door, she bent down and said, "You don't fight fair."

CHAPTER 4

*S*olomon had no intention of fighting fair where Larissa was concerned. He was curious about this woman and wanted to know all about her. He just had to figure out a way to make that happen while living in California. Because he intended to be on the first available flight home.

But the next morning, he received a call from Bob Harding, one of the senior partners at his firm, that made him realize just how determined his absentee father was to keep him where he didn't want to be.

"Good morning, Mr. Harding, sir," Solomon greeted him. "How are things going back home?"

"Everything is going well, Solomon. As a matter of fact, I'm on my way into a meeting to discuss another multimillion-dollar account that our firm is in good position to take over."

"That's great news. And don't worry—I'll be back soon to help facilitate."

"There's no need for you to rush back," Harding said.

"I'm no slacker, sir. If we have a new account coming in, I should be there to help. I don't mind cutting my vacation short." Solomon was so ready to get out of North Carolina that he would gladly handle the grunt work on that new account. He'd do just about anything to avoid having to hang around here another day.

"I don't think you understand what I'm saying." Harding cleared his throat. "The reason I'm calling is because your father has just put the firm on retainer. He wants you to stay in Charlotte for a while in order to help him with a pending case. So, you are no longer on vacation."

Oh, this was not happening. "I hope you didn't just loan me out without at least talking to me first." Solomon felt his nostrils flare. He'd being weighing his options all night long, which was the reason he hadn't booked his flight the moment he'd gotten back to his hotel room last night. But by that morning, Solomon had all but decided to book that flight. That his father would go behind his back in order to force him to take his case aggravated him to the nth degree.

"Look at it from our perspective, Son."

Solomon shook his head. He didn't need another old man calling him "Son" while trying to get him to do something he didn't want any part of.

"Pastor Davison is like royalty in the South," Harding continued. "He has his own television broadcasts, he writes books, and he produces Christian films. This case is perfect for our firm."

Yeah, but is it perfect for me? "What if he's guilty?" Solomon asked.

"What if he is? Our job is not to wonder why, it's to get the jury to wonder 'what if?'" Harding reminded him.

"I hardly know my father, so I'm just not sure if I want to get involved."

"Be that as it may, the firm is very interested in the case."

"Bottom line, sir. Are you ordering me to take this case?"

"I wouldn't call it an 'order'…maybe more like a strong suggestion that you act in the interests of the firm. It could pay off for you in the long run."

They always hinted at his eventual promotion to partner whenever they wanted him to do something that went against his preferences or his convictions. "And you're not worried about the firm's image, in the event that Pastor Davison actually did this thing he's been accused of doing?"

Harding sighed. "I don't understand your obsession with representing the wrongly accused versus the rightly accused."

"Fine, I'll take the case," Solomon conceded. "But I'm giving you fair warning: If this client turns out to be as guilty as sin, then you'll have my resignation on your desk when I return."

"That'll be the worst mistake of your career. Look, I don't know what problems you are having with your father, but you need to remember that our firm is committed to offering its clients the best possible defense."

"Some people need to pay for their wrongdoings."

"Not if they have the money to pay for a defense that our firm provides. So, the only thing I need to know is what help you'll need from us to get the job done for our new client."

Solomon was beginning to think that he no longer fit in at People, Smith, and Harding. He didn't want to represent someone simply because he or she was willing to pay whatever it took to mount a credible defense. Solomon was more of a crusader, out looking for his next cause…the next unjustly accused man or woman. There were too many people spending years behind bars for crimes they didn't commit, all because they lacked adequate funds for a competent attorney. Solomon had a passion for those kinds of cases and strongly believed that God had blessed him with the ability to fight for justice for those people.

All of this "helping those who had the money to help themselves" business was not in his plans. "The only thing I'm requesting for this job is Lamar Stevens," he told Harding.

"Do you really need to pull one of our best private detectives for this case?"

"That's what I need, sir."

"Okay, we'll fly him down there. Just try not to keep him too long, okay?"

"I'll do my best."

After hanging up, Solomon took a quick shower and put on his navy blue suit. He was going to the hospital to see his father, but he wanted there to be no mistake—the purpose of this visit was strictly business.

At the hospital, Solomon entered his father's room and sat down in a chair next to the bed. He didn't bother to ask how he was feeling; he just pulled out his iPad and tapped the notepad icon. "Okay, you're paying for my time, so let's get to it."

"Good morning to you, too, Son. How was your evening? Did you enjoy dinner with Larissa?"

Practically glaring at his father, Solomon said through clenched teeth, "I do not want to be here. But I want to be here even less when you call me 'Son.' So, if you truly need me to handle this case for you, I would like to be called Solomon and nothing else. Okay?"

"I apologize," David said sincerely. "I know I haven't earned the right to call you that. But I do hope to earn the right one day. Will you at least give me the chance to do that while you're here?"

"Let's just keep things the way they've been…you act like you don't have a son named Solomon, and I live like I don't have a father in my life. That way, neither one of us will become confused. Now, back to business." Solomon glanced down at the list of questions he'd compiled. "What is the full name of your accuser and her daughter?"

"My accuser's name is Summer Jones, and the child goes by the name Winter Sawyer."

"You're kidding, right?"

David shook his head. "Serious. Those are their names."

"So, what, is the grandmother named Spring?"

"Don't make me laugh—you know I'm recovering from a heart attack. I have to take it easy."

"Sorry about that. Okay then, we have Summer and Winter." Solomon typed a note. "How long were they attending the church before they sought counseling?"

"Do me a favor, Solomon. Can you at least look at me from time to time while asking your questions?"

Solomon knew he was being childish by keeping his eyes averted from his father as much as possible. He might be forced to be at his father's side, but he wasn't there as kin; he was there as a lawyer, and he didn't want his involvement with the family to extend beyond a business relationship.

When the door opened and Larissa walked in wearing a white jacket with a stethoscope around her neck, Solomon revised his thoughts. He wouldn't mind getting involved with this member of the family. "Don't you look nice and official this morning?" he asked her.

"I wasn't on duty yesterday, but a woman's gotta work sometime." She looked at David. "I thought I'd check on you while I'm on break."

He beamed. "You worry about me too much. You should be in that cafeteria drinking coffee and letting some handsome doctor take notice of you."

She shook her head as she approached his bedside. "Believe it or not, Uncle David, the highlight of my life was not figuring out which dress to wear to prom. Nor do I take much pleasure in being ogled by strangers, whether they are doctors or not. So, you can quit trying to marry me off so soon."

"So soon? You're almost thirty."

"I'm twenty-seven, thank you very much. And I'm enjoying my life just the way it is."

He sighed. "I don't know why you have to be the difficult one. All I want is for all my children to be happy. You may be enjoying your career now, but there will come a day when you'll want someone by your side."

Larissa bent down and kissed him on the forehead. "Like Auntie has been by your side."

He nodded. "Not a day goes by that I don't thank God for your auntie. She's been a better wife to me than I have been a husband to her."

"I think she would disagree with you on that," Larissa said. "All I've ever heard her say is how blessed she was for meeting you."

David smiled and turned to Solomon. "Did you hear that?"

"I heard it," he grunted. "What do you want me to do, give you a cookie?"

"No cookies for him," Larissa said, rolling her eyes at Solomon. "He's on the mend, and I don't want him having any setbacks from eating a bunch of stuff he has no business eating."

"Calm down, Larissa. I was just joking," Solomon told her.

"You were just being rude. But it's okay; Uncle David can handle you."

"You think I can take him?" David asked. "Maybe box his ears for sassing me?" He punched the air with his fists.

"I know you can," Larissa said. "Solomon is all talk." She looked at him and stuck out her tongue, then returned her attention to her uncle. "Even on your sickbed, you'd be able to shut him down."

"I think you'd better quit messing with me, Solomon." David playfully shook a fist in his face. "That is, if you don't want me to get up and use these lethal weapons."

Solomon shook his head. "Okay, well, can you put that lethal weapon down and finish answering my questions so I can do the job you're paying me to do?" This man was in danger of losing everything he'd worked for, and all he wanted to do was make jokes.

Larissa pulled up a chair. "So, you decided to take the case? That's wonderful news. I'm so happy."

Solomon was about to make an offhanded comment about how her precious uncle had strong-armed him by calling his boss before he could make up his mind, but Larissa was looking at him as if she thought he'd hung the moon. All he managed to say was, "Yeah, looks like I'll be hanging around a little while longer."

"Thank you, Solomon. I really appreciate it." She grinned. "Let me know if there's anything I can do to help."

Oh, he could think of a few things she could do to help him, like doing dinner and a movie. Or she could let him kiss her again. He doubted that she would go for any of those things, though, so he just said, "I'll keep that in mind." Then he turned back to David. "Okay, let's get back at it. You never told me how long Summer and Winter were members at the church before the counseling began."

David thought for a bit before answering. "I think they joined about a month before Summer started calling the church or catching me after service to ask if I would help with her daughter."

"How many times did she reach out to you before you agreed to do it?"

"I don't think I ever agreed to do it, exactly."

"What do you mean?" Solomon was confused.

"He means that he got roped into it by my cousin," Larissa answered.

David frowned. "Adam didn't rope me into it. I asked Summer to check with the elders and ask if any of them could put her on their calendar. But Adam brought her back to me because the elders' calendars were already full, and he thought that this family needed immediate help."

"That's when Uncle David pulled me in," Larissa said. Just then, Alma walked into the room. Larissa stood up and hugged her. "I was wondering where you were."

Alma smiled. "David is being released today, so I was at home getting everything in order for him."

"I hope you got yourself a good night's sleep," David said to his wife. "And I don't want you fussing over me at home. As a matter of fact, I had Leah plan a spa day for you."

Alma stared at him, wide-eyed. "David Davison, have you lost your mind? I can't just go off for a massage and facial while you are still on the mend." She turned to Larissa. "Did you know about this?"

Larissa shook her head and held up her hands. "I didn't have anything to do with it."

"You can go, and you will go, woman," David declared. "You've been at this hospital night and day. Go do something for yourself. I promise I'm not dying anytime soon. Okay?"

Alma seemed completely flustered by this turn of events. She looked around the room, turned back to her husband, and threw her hands in the air. "If I go to the, how are you going to get home? Larissa can't leave the hospital. She doesn't get off until six."

David pointed at Solomon. "He can take me home. We're working on this case, anyway. We can spend the day putting our heads together as we try to figure out our approach."

Alma frowned. "I'm not sure about this, David."

"Stop being a worrywart, Alma. Solomon can take care of me while you're out for the day. It would make me happy if you did this for yourself."

"As long as you all have this handled, I'm headed back to work," Larissa said, walking toward the door. Just before leaving, she said, "I'll see you at the house this evening, Uncle David."

Solomon had been about to object to the plan of him spending the day with Pastor Davison, but Larissa's announcement that she would be coming to the house when she got off work made him decide to just sit back and see where the day would lead.

CHAPTER 5

*W*hy didn't you just call one of your kids to come hang out with you today?" Solomon asked as he handed David the pillow and blanket he'd requested.

David thanked him but didn't answer his question, instead working on getting comfortable on the sectional in the family room.

"I just don't understand why Adam or one of your daughters isn't here with you," Solomon persisted. "They all know that you were released from the hospital today, don't they?"

"Yes, they know, but they have busy lives, and Adam is busy taking care of things at church while I'm recovering." David fluffed his pillow, then leaned back against it. "But I like this...just you and me hanging out. I used to have dreams about going places and doing things with you. God has been good to me, and I thank Him for giving us this time together."

Solomon was caught off guard by his father's remarks. He'd always assumed that the pastor never gave him a second thought after sending his monthly child support check. Actually, Solomon had assumed that he would have tasked an accountant with taking care of that rather than tending to it personally.

"What?" David asked, and Solomon realized he'd been staring at him. "Are you surprised that I have feelings for the son I never knew? That it bothered me not to be around you all those years?"

"Actually, yeah," Solomon admitted.

"Well, it shouldn't," David said. "You may not like looking at me, but I'm so thankful to God that I am able to look you in the face today and tell you that I never forgot about you. Not a day went by that I didn't pray to God for your safety and for the day when you and I would finally come together as father and son."

"That would be a lot easier for me to believe if you had just once showed an interest in me when I was a kid…when I needed you most."

"I showed more of an interest than you know."

"Mmpf," Solomon muttered, incredulous.

"Well, if you're not going to talk to your old man, why don't you turn on the television so we can have something to occupy us?"

Solomon picked up the remote control and turned on the TV. He began channel-surfing while David gave a running commentary on which shows he liked and which shows he wouldn't waste his time on. "Shows like Andy Griffith and Bill Cosby's just aren't being produced anymore," he lamented. "If it's not scandalous, I guess people don't want to watch it."

"I catch the news pretty routinely and watch a movie every now and then," Solomon said. "Other than that, I don't watch much TV." He finally settled on the Travel Channel. *Man v. Food* was on.

"Alma likes this guy," David said, pointing at the screen. "Every time she watches his show, she says, 'This guy is working on a heart attack. I hope he exercises.' And here, I have a heart attack, even though I work out and try to eat healthy most of the time. I know I'm living right."

"That's debatable," Solomon told him. But this remark didn't stem from anger. He had slipped into a place of comfort and was actually beginning to almost enjoy this time spent with the father he'd never had a chance to know.

David nodded. "I certainly haven't been perfect, especially where you were concerned. I only pray that you'll be able to forgive me someday."

"So, what are you saying?" Solomon asked. "Because I'm confused. Did you ask me to come down here to be your legal counsel, or do you want to have a relationship with me?"

"Son—I mean, Solomon—I could hire an attorney in North Carolina if I just wanted an attorney. I need you in my life, and I'm thankful that Alma and I finally came to an agreement on that."

"Oh yeah, that's right. You were able to keep your marriage as long as you agreed to never be a father to me."

David squirmed a bit. "Things were different back then. Alma was mortified over what I had done to her and to our marriage. The only way she was able to forgive me was to pretend none of it ever happened."

"And she's okay with me being here now?"

David nodded. "We've both grown to the point where all we want to do is make each other happy. She's a good woman, Solomon. If you give her a chance, I think you'll love her like a second mother, or, if not that, then a very close friend."

Solomon didn't know about that. Alma had taken from him the only thing he'd lacked during his childhood years. What if she suddenly decided that she didn't want Solomon around anymore? Will he be banished to no-man's-land again? He tried to take his mind off the thoughts bombarding his mind as he watched a rerun of *Law and*

Order. His father fell asleep halfway through the second episode, and Solomon noticed that the blanket was falling off him. He got up to fix it and stood there for a moment, staring at the man he so closely resembled. The man he knew so little about. He pulled the blanket over his father's chest, then sat back down, trying to get his emotions in check.

Several minutes later, Solomon's phone rang. He glanced at the screen and saw that it was Lamar Stevens, so he went to the kitchen to take the call. "Hey, Lamar," he answered. "Thanks for getting back to me so soon."

"I hear I'm getting an all-expenses-paid trip to the South."

"Do you mind? I could really use your help. I doubt if it would take you more than a few days."

"I can't seem to get any of these Hollywood starlets to give me the time of day, so I might as well come out there and try my luck with some of those beauty queens in Charlotte."

Solomon chuckled. "You better watch yourself. Don't come down here and get a restraining order put on you."

Lamar laughed. "Very funny. I'll have you know that the ladies love me everywhere but in LA. For some reason, these wannabes think that being a private investigator is something akin to a roach."

"I really can't say if it's much better in the South, because I'm getting the Raid treatment from a lovely lady I just met down here."

"That's because you don't have no rap. I've seen you try to push up on the honeys. Take it from me—you need some player lessons."

"Forget all that. I don't have problems with the ladies."

Lamar smacked his lips. "I'm just saying…you might want to open that Bible and read about the dude you were named after. Now, *that* Solomon had some player moves."

"Even if I wanted to learn about such things, I don't have time in my life for all the women King Solomon had. I'll be satisfied if I can find just one woman to love."

"Is that right?"

Solomon spun around and came face-to-face with Larissa. "I'll see you when you get here, Lamar." He ended the call, then said, "Do you think it was right to sneak up on me and eavesdrop on my conversation?"

She laughed. "Eavesdrop? Right. You wish I was eavesdropping on you. I just walked into the kitchen and heard you talking. Is that a crime?"

He was smiling at her as he said, "I'm sure I can find a precedent in the law books."

"Search as long as you like—I'm positive you won't find anything to charge me with." She put her hands on her hips and added, "But I bet there is something in those law books of yours about kissing a woman without first getting her permission."

Solomon propped his elbows on the counter of the kitchen island, enjoying every second he took to study Larissa. She was a work of art, perfection defined, right before his eyes. But it was obvious to him now that she had spent way too much time in the books and hardly any time dating. "I'd sure hate for you to call what I did last night a kiss."

"You did kiss me," she insisted, indignant.

Shaking his head, Solomon stepped away from the island and came to stand in front of her. He bent down and whispered in her ear, "When I really kiss you, you'll know the difference."

Larissa backed away from him. "I didn't come over here to spar with you. How is Uncle David doing?"

Solomon pointed to the family room. "He's asleep in there. But you know what I don't get?"

Larissa folded her arms across her chest. "I'm sure you're going to tell me."

He ignored the sarcasm. "He has three children, but none of them showed up or even called since he's been home. You're the first one."

Larissa dropped her arms at her sides. "Uncle David and I have a special relationship. He's like a father to me. Tamara and Leah are still a little upset with him over his recent announcement, but they'll get over it."

"You mean, they're upset about me. As if I asked to be here."

"Not just about you," Larissa whispered. "They're also upset over how all of this was kept hidden from them."

"And they think I'm not?" Solomon wanted to get on the first thing smoking and hightail it back to LA. He didn't need this. If his brothers and sisters didn't want anything to do with him, then he would just go on living life the way he'd lived it before his father's heart attack. "And what about Adam? How does he feel about me?"

"I haven't had a chance to talk to Adam. He's busy handling things at the church. But you can go there and talk to him tonight, if you want. We have Bible study on Wednesdays."

"I just might do that. So, are you going to Bible study?"

"I'll hang around here until Aunt Alma gets back, and then I'll meet you over there, if you'd like."

"That sounds good," Solomon said. "I might need your help getting an audience with my brother. I have a few questions for him about Summer Jones."

"Okay. Well, I should go check on Uncle David."

"Yeah, he might need you to change the TV channel for him."

Larissa laughed. "Men. When you get sick or injured, you're such babies."

Larissa practically danced into the family room and plopped down on the sectional, smiling dreamily. There was something about Solomon that she found extremely attractive. He was handsome and charming when he wanted to be, and he had a way of making her forget herself when she was around him.

"What are you grinning about? Still thinking about that kiss?"

Larissa jumped. "Uncle David! I thought you were still asleep."

"How could I sleep with you and Solomon carrying on in the kitchen?"

"And he called *me* an eavesdropper. You are terrible, Uncle David! You're supposed to be in here resting, not spying on others. And it wasn't a kiss."

"Oh, that's what he said, but you know that's just a ploy to get you to let him kiss you again, right?" David chuckled. "That's my son. I used to have a way with the ladies myself, back in the day."

"Well, he doesn't have a way with me. He's my cousin, and that's that."

"Didn't that boy tell you enough times already that he's not your kin?"

"You're my uncle," she reminded him.

"I sure am. And you're more like a daughter to me than a niece. I still remember the first day you came to stay with us." His eyes took on a faraway look. "You were so afraid of us that you stayed in your room the first week. You spoke only when spoken to, and when you did speak, it was just a tiny whisper. *Just like this*," he whispered.

Larissa loved her uncle because he had shown her patience and love when she'd needed them the most. At ten, her father had been sent to prison for armed robbery, and her mother had checked herself into rehab. Both had promised Larissa that her time with Alma and David would be short, because they would come back for her as soon as they could. But her father's twelve-year sentence changed all of that. Her mother dropped out of rehab and hadn't been heard from since.

"You've been good to me," Larissa said, "better than any father could have ever been." She leaned over and hugged her uncle. "Thank you."

"You don't have to thank me. It was my pleasure to watch you grow into the incredible woman you turned out to be. I'm the one who should be thanking you. Because, in a way, raising you helped me to put aside the guilt I felt for not being able to raise Solomon. I used to promise God that I was going to take special care of you and raise you up until that special man came into your life and took my place. And I asked God to watch over my son just like I was watching over you."

"If that's the case, then I can guarantee you that Solomon lacked for nothing."

"Except for the love of his father," he said with a look of conviction on his face.

Larissa put her hand on his shoulder. "Don't beat yourself up over it, Uncle David. What's done is done. All we can do is move forward now."

Nodding, Uncle David said, "I know that in my head, but I'm having a hard time convincing my heart, especially when Solomon looks at me as if I stole something from him."

"I'm working on him, so don't worry." She grinned. "I'll have Solomon singing your praises in no time."

"Oh, so that's why you're going on a Bible study date with him tonight—to help me?" David smirked.

"You were just pretending to be asleep the whole time, weren't you?" Larissa shook her head. "What am I going to do with you?" Then she laughed at his antics. "I'll have you know that I'm going to church tonight to be a go-between for your two sons."

Her uncle sobered. "Thanks for doing that, Rissa. I'm hoping that once Solomon feels a part of this family, he'll warm up to his old man."

After her conversation that afternoon with Leah and Tamara, Larissa doubted that any of them would be hugging and smiling and coming together as a family unit anytime soon. But she wouldn't upset her uncle with that knowledge. So, she just smiled at him and said, "I'll do my best."

CHAPTER 6

"What took you so long?" Solomon asked as Larissa strutted in through the back door of the church looking as if the sun was made so it could shine on her and her alone.

"I told you I was going to stay with Uncle David until my aunt came back home," she said. "You didn't have to wait on me. You could have gone to the sanctuary for praise and worship."

"I wasn't just standing around waiting on you because I was afraid to go into the sanctuary. I have something to show you." Solomon wasn't about to let Larissa get it twisted. She was beautiful, and yes, he had designs on her. But it wasn't as if he couldn't live without her. At least, that was what he wanted to get across to her.

"Can't it wait until after service?" she asked. "Adam will be getting up to preach soon."

Solomon shook his head. "No, it's urgent. Is there a room where we can go? I think we need some privacy for what I'm about to show you."

Larissa led him to the prayer room, where they sat down on a sofa. "What's up?" she asked.

Solomon turned on his iPad and passed it to her. "The church secretary did a blog post asking for prayer for David."

"Yeah, I know. I asked her to do that." Larissa was holding the iPad in her hand but hadn't looked at it yet.

"Well, the responses to her blog post have gone viral. And you need to see what's being said."

As Larissa began reading the comments that had been left on the church's blog site, the look on her face went from shocked to stricken to horrified. Solomon could almost tell which post she was reading and when. *"I'll pray that he repents so that he can meet his maker with a clean conscience,"* one person had said. Another comment read, *"These preachers think they can live high on the hog while the rest of us barely get by. And then, when one of them gets what's coming to him, the first thing he does is ask us to pray for him."*

Looking to Solomon with sorrow-filled eyes, Larissa asked, "Has the world really become this hateful?"

"It's worse than you know. I have dealt with some real characters." He pointed at the iPad. "Did you read comment number six?"

"I didn't read past the first three. I don't think I could stomach any more of this." Larissa handed the device back to him.

"It's not all bad," he assured her, pushing the iPad toward her again. "Most of the people who responded said that they're praying for your uncle. They're even refuting some of the rude comments. But you really need to read comment number six."

Sighing deeply, Larissa did as Solomon requested. She was indeed looking sick as she read, *"I do believe it is our duty to pray for our spiritual leaders. But I don't like hypocrites. And I certainly won't be praying for a man who cheats on his wife and leaves fatherless children from coast to coast."*

Larissa's mouth dropped open. She met Solomon's eyes. "They wouldn't have!"

"Who else if not your wonderful cousins? It's not as if David spread the good news about his illegitimate son. None of you knew anything about me until this week."

"But why would they do this? What would they have to gain from it?"

Solomon shrugged one shoulder. "Maybe it's not what they have to gain that inspired this comment but what David told them they could lose."

"Can you please stop calling him 'David'? He's your father, for crying out loud."

"Looks to me like he was more of a father to you than he ever was to me," Solomon said. "So, if you don't mind, I'll stick with 'Pastor Davison' or simply 'David.'"

Larissa shook her head, then put her hand on Solomon's shoulder. "If my cousins posted that comment, then I'd like to apologize to you on their behalf. Their animosity toward you is only making it harder for you to develop a relationship with your father."

"You don't ever need to apologize to me, Larissa. You've treated me better than anyone in this family."

Smirking, Larissa said, "I thought we weren't family."

For the first time since reading those awful comments online, Solomon smiled. "Don't get carried away. I only meant that you are a part of them. But if you and I were family, I wouldn't be able to do this, now, would I?" He wrapped his arms around her and leaned in for a kiss.

Larissa pushed him back. "Please. We are in church, in case you didn't notice." She stood up. "Come on. Let's grab a seat in the sanctuary so we can hear the Word of God."

Solomon wanted to stay just where he was and try his best to convince Larissa that God didn't have anything against kissing. But he could tell that Larissa wasn't in the mood to listen, so he got up and followed her into the sanctuary.

Adam presented himself well. He looked like a preacher as he stood behind the pulpit and argued the case for God. Solomon tried to imagine how his father's booming voice would sound from that pulpit. If Adam was any indication, then David Davison must be something else. It struck him then that he himself was an indication. In high school and college, his teachers and professors had told him that he was a skilled orator. It was his gift of gab and his ability to argue persuasively that had made many people encourage him to attend law school. All this time, Solomon had assumed he possessed those abilities because he'd studied and worked at them. But what if his interest in public speaking and arguing cases had come from his father? Solomon leaned back in his seat. "I don't believe it," he murmured under his breath as Adam delivered his closing point.

"You don't believe what?" Larissa whispered.

Solomon looked at her. "Sorry. I didn't realize I said that out loud."

Everyone rose for the benediction, then Larissa pulled on Solomon's arm. "Come on; let's go talk to Adam. Hopefully he won't ask you about his message, since you obviously weren't paying attention to it."

<hr />

"Spying on me?" Adam asked as Solomon and Larissa took a seat before his desk.

"I'm sure I don't know what you're talking about," Solomon replied.

"Don't pretend with me. I know that Daddy sent you here to check up on me. Well, you can go back to the house and tell the old man that his firstborn is preaching the Word just as he was taught."

Solomon nearly jumped out of the chair. "I came tonight because I was interested to discover how you felt about my presence here. I think I've received my answer. So, I'll just see myself out."

"Wait a minute." Larissa grabbed hold of his hand. "Don't leave like this." She turned to Adam. "And you need to stop acting like a two-year-old. We all need to work together in order to help your father."

Solomon's nostrils flared—and so did Adam's. Larissa blinked in disbelief, looking from one man to the other and back again. She couldn't believe she was just now realizing how closely they resembled each other. Their eyes were shaped the same; they had the same skin tone and high cheekbones. Even their noses were similar—small and a little crooked, tilting toward the left. And they were both stubborn as the day is long.

Larissa was beginning to think she might need to call Uncle David and have him tell his sons to place nice. But then a miracle happened, appropriately, in the house of God. Adam relented. "Okay, you're right," he said. "Sit back down and let's reason with one another."

Larissa turned to Solomon, who appeared as if he was ready to oblige. She put her hand in his and squeezed. "You can do this. Come on. Sit down and let's get this over with."

Solomon squeezed her hand back, then sat down and got right to business. "I need to ask you a few questions about the Jones family," he said to Adam.

"I'm sure we have several Jones families in attendance at our church," Adam said, narrowing his eyes. "Can you be a bit more specific?"

"Obviously, I'm not asking about some random Jones family at this church. I'm asking you about Summer Jones and her daughter, Winter

Sawyer—the people who are trying to sue your father. Do you remember them?"

"No need to be sarcastic—of course I remember them." Adam shrugged. "What do you want to know?"

"For starters, can you tell us why you asked Pastor David to counsel them instead of doing it yourself? From what I was told, Summer Jones approached you first."

Adam turned to Larissa. The look in his eyes accused her of being a traitor. When she'd told her uncle that she would help these two communicate with each other, the idea had seemed a lot simpler than the reality. "I didn't divulge any confidences, Adam, so stop looking at me like that. You did ask Uncle David to counsel that family."

"Well, I had my reasons," Adam said.

"And what were those reasons?" Solomon countered.

Adam folded his arms over his chest. "None of your business."

Solomon stood up again. "This is a waste of my time. I will get the answers I need from another source."

Larissa got up and followed him out of the office. He was walking fast, so she had to jog to catch up with him. "Hey, wait a minute." She grabbed his arm once they reached the fellowship hall. "I can't believe you're giving up so soon. We didn't even ask him about the comment that was posted on the Internet about you."

"Did you see him in there?" Solomon pointed in the direction of Adam's office. "He's a closed book. I wouldn't be able to get him to give me the time of day, let alone answers to specific questions. We'll just need to work this out another way."

"So what are you proposing?"

Solomon took hold of Larissa's hand. "I have the perfect person for the job. Come with me."

Solomon shook hands with his buddy Lamar Stevens, lead investigator for People, Smith, and Harding, when he picked him up at the airport.

"Good seeing you, bro," Lamar said. "I thought you were going to leave me to sleep here."

"You know me better than that," Solomon said as he loaded his friend's suitcases into the trunk. "I had to take care of a little business before I picked you up. But don't worry; your hotel room is ready and waiting for you."

Larissa was seated up front, so Lamar climbed in back, and Solomon made the introductions.

"Are all the women in Charlotte as lovely as you?" Lamar asked while shaking Larissa's hand.

"No," Solomon answered for her. "And Larissa's not the kind of woman who would fall for any of your tired ol' player moves. So, let go of her hand, or I'll let you out right here so you'll have to wait on a taxi."

"Ah, man, you never were any fun." Lamar shook his head and leaned back in his seat. "I can see right now that I need to hurry my investigation along so I can get out of this town."

"You don't have to leave so soon," Larissa chirped. "I have two cousins I can introduce you to. Both are lovely. You're bound to hit it off with one of them."

"I doubt it," Solomon said with a scowl. "After spending two minutes with either one of them, you'd be pulling out that can of Raid."

Lamar laughed. "They can't be that bad."

"You don't know the half of it."

Larissa gave Solomon a gentle slap on his arm. "Hush up, Solomon. They aren't that bad." She turned to Lamar. "They also happen to be

Solomon's half sisters. He just met them, but I think he's already getting to be a tad bit overprotective of them."

"In your dreams." Solomon rolled his eyes and then changed the subject. "Look, man, I'm glad you're here. We are getting absolutely nowhere on this case."

"You might be nowhere, but I've already uncovered some pretty interesting information about Little Ms. Spring."

"Summer," Solomon said.

"Close enough." Lamar shrugged. "I knew it had something to do with the seasons."

CHAPTER 7

The Worship Center of God had a little over ten thousand members, thirty deacons, and eleven elders. At this very moment, Adam was meeting with the elders to explain to them why they were no longer able to reach Pastor David. "I'm sure you all can understand that my father needs to rest right now. His condition is serious."

"I talked to David just yesterday," said Elder Watts, the head elder and best friend of Adam's father. "He told me to call anytime I need him."

"That was before my mother noticed the strain those calls were putting on him."

"What about the issues we've been dealing with lately?" another elder called out. "Church members have approached all of us with allegations of an affair that Pastor David supposedly had. If we can't talk to him, then how will we know how to respond?"

Adam looked to his wife, Portia. When she had shown up at the church that morning, he had been ticked off, because she hadn't made it to the hospital even once to check on his ailing father. But when she gave him a confident nod and then turned to the elder, prepared to address the question for which Adam had no answer, he was grateful that his wife had decided to come.

"Your response is simple," Portia said. "Pastor David Davison is a dedicated Christian who loves his wife, his family, and his church. He would never do anything to harm any of them."

"That sounds real good on a press release," said Elder Johnson, "but we're talking about church members who have Facebook accounts and who surf the net and can easily find out about this upcoming lawsuit."

"And what's this business about David having a bunch of illegitimate children?" Elder Wilson added.

Adam rolled his eyes. "You can't believe everything you read, Elder Wilson. If that was the case, then we'd all be convinced that your son was a Peeping Tom, as the newspapers reported a few months back."

"Let me remind you that my son was cleared of those charges," the elder fumed. "And you have no right to bring that up in a public meeting like this."

"He has every right," Portia proclaimed. "Let *me* remind *you* that Pastor Davison's wife has asked Adam to sacrifice extra time and energy, not to mention the time with his family, so that he can head this ministry and give my father-in-law a fair chance at recovery."

"What does that mean for us?" Elder Watts asked. He turned to Adam. "Do we report to you now?"

Adam nodded, trying to keep his face as straight as possible, even though his mouth wanted to curve into a smile. He wouldn't want to be accused of being too happy. "That is what my mother requested."

"Well, what does your father want?" Elder Calvin asked. "I mean, he's still the senior pastor, after all."

Adam did allow himself to smile then. All of these men thought they were so superior to him. They were always whispering behind his back, telling others that he held the position of associate pastor just because his father was the senior pastor. But Adam was about to show all of them. They would either roll with him or get rolled over.

⌒⌒⌒

"Can you help me understand how meeting with your children will get anything resolved?" Solomon asked David. "They have been completely unhelpful to the process thus far." He was a quick study, and he had learned his lesson about dealing with his half siblings.

"Son."

Solomon flinched.

"I'm sorry." David put his hand on top of Solomon's. "I know it bothers you when I call you that. I'll try to be more aware. But do me a favor and help an old man out."

Solomon forced a smile. "What do you want me to do now?"

"Give me a hint or something when I'm cleared to call you 'Son,' because I really like how that sounds."

For a moment, Solomon and his father stared at each other, neither one saying anything or acknowledging that a connection was being made. Then Larissa entered the family room carrying a tray of hors d'oeuvres; Alma trailed behind with a pitcher of iced tea. Solomon was only too happy to change the subject. "Do you really think that feeding them will entice them to confess?"

Alma sat down next to Solomon. "I have faith in my children. They may be angry with their father right now, but I don't think they want to destroy his legacy."

"If you say so." Solomon wasn't so sure. His extended family members didn't seem pleased about his presence one bit, but would they destroy everything their father had built over an almost thirty-year-old sin? The jury was still out on that one.

The front door opened, and Adam and Tamara walked in. Alma left his side and rushed to greet her children with hugs and kisses, once again making Solomon feel like a second-class citizen.

Larissa took the spot that Alma had abandoned. She put her hand on Solomon's arm. "Are you okay?"

Solomon turned to her and nodded. "Of course. Why wouldn't I be?"

Larissa leaned forward to see around him. "And how are you doing today, Uncle David?" she asked.

"I'm doing better than Alma thinks. If she puts one more blanket over me, I'm going start having hot flashes."

"What do you know about hot flashes?" Alma asked as she sat down on the arm of David's lounge chair. "I don't think men should speak of things they have never experienced."

"I know a lot about them," David insisted. "Every night when one of those flashes hits, somebody in this house"—he nudged Alma with his elbow—"throws the covers off, like I'm going to do now." Then he lifted the three layers of blankets from his lap and moved them to the side, stretching out his legs.

Alma's hands went to her hips. "David Davison. I will not stand by and watch you catch your death of cold. You know that it's much cooler down here than it is upstairs."

Solomon saw genuine anxiety on Alma's face, and he looked to David to see if he even noticed how concerned this woman was for him.

David peeled one of the blankets away from the other two and put it back around his legs. "There," he said to his wife. "I put one blanket on, and if I get cold, I promise to put the others on, as well." Alma relaxed her posture and smiled down at David, who gently rubbed her back. "Stop worrying so much about me, Alma, or you're bound to come down with something yourself. The last thing I need is for you to get sick."

The front door opened again. "Where are you guys?" Leah yelled.

"We're in the family room," Adam shouted back.

"Hey, everybody," Leah said as she rushed into the room looking like she had a million and one things on her mind. "I hope this won't take long. I left a mountain of paperwork on my desk, and I simply must get back."

"You know I don't like you working at the church late into the night by yourself," David admonished her.

"Relax, Dad. The choir is rehearsing tonight, so I'll have plenty of company."

"Okay, well, now that we're all together..." Alma stood up to address them. "Your father and I need to talk with you all about something that has come to our attention." She glanced at her husband, and he winked at her, so she continued. "Yesterday, someone posted a comment on the Internet about something that only the seven of us know about. This information was made to sound like more than it is, and it has the potential to damage the reputation of our ministry."

"Why don't you just spit it out, Mama?" Tamara sneered. "I read the comment, and I'm sure the rest of you read it, as well." Her eyes roved the room. "Someone said Daddy has kids all over the country."

"Which is not true," Alma stated emphatically.

"How do we know it's not true?" Leah asked her. "You're not with Daddy every second of the day. Who knows what he does when you're not around?"

"Leah!" Larissa looked astonished and saddened. "What's wrong with you? Why are you speaking against your own father like this?"

But Leah wasn't backing down. "Why not? My new brother"—she pointed at Solomon—"is the perfect example. Daddy kept quiet about him for all these years. So, I ask again," she said, turning to her mother, "how do you know that Daddy didn't do what he's being accused of?"

Alma sighed. "I know it, and that's all that matters. And I will not tolerate any of you speaking ill of my husband. Do you understand?"

"Well, I don't have anything good to say right now, so maybe I should just leave." Leah stood up, glaring at her mother.

"Maybe you should." Alma didn't even give it a second's thought. "You need to work on your attitude, Leah. Maybe you should forget about the work at church and just go home to your apartment to pray about the way you've been acting."

David pushed himself up in his lounge chair. "Now, wait a minute, Alma. Don't go throwing the kids out. It's not Leah's fault. She has every right to be upset with me."

"Not today, she doesn't," Alma said, still staring her eldest daughter down as she pointed in the direction of the front door.

Leah stormed out of the room as quickly as she had entered it.

Solomon was struck by how protective Alma was of David. She loved this man, and he believed that David loved her. And it was in that moment, as he looked from Alma to David and back again, that he realized Alma had every reason to trust her husband. Solomon was catching the fever, too, because he was beginning to believe that David Davison would not risk his marriage for a silly fling with a troubled youth.

Alma still had the floor. She faced her remaining two children and said, "Look, let's keep it simple. I want to know which one of you posted that horrible comment about your father."

"It wasn't me," Tamara said with a shrug. "I would never say anything like that about Daddy."

Crossing his arms over his chest, Adam said, "Don't look at me. I don't like this situation any more than the next person, but I would never put our business out there like that."

"What about Portia?" Tamara asked. "I wouldn't put it past that snake to do something like this. She's probably writing a tell-all book about the family as we speak."

"Leave my wife out of this," Adam groused. "She's not a snake, and for your information, she helped me fend off questions about that crazy blog."

"I heard that from Elder Watts," David said. "He called right after the meeting. It's a good thing Portia was there with you."

Adam rolled his eyes. "I asked Elder Watts not to call you. I told all of them that Mama wants you to rest."

David waved the comment off. "I called Eugene myself. You know that he and I have a standing golf game, and I wanted to make sure he was keeping up with it, even though I'm laid up for a little while."

"If you kids didn't write that comment, then who did?" Alma said, getting back on topic. "It's not as if your father or I told anyone else about Solomon."

"Why do you assume it was one of us?" Tamara asked her. "Why don't you question Larissa? Or Solomon himself? Maybe one of them did it."

Larissa shook her head and turned her gaze heavenward. "Why would I do something like that?"

Tamara rolled her eyes. "You can pretend to be innocent if you want, but you're the one cozying up to Solomon. Who knows what kind of scheme the two of you are cooking up? Maybe you want Daddy to have another heart attack so you can hurry up and collect your inheritance."

"Tamara Davison! That was not called for." Alma narrowed her eyes at her daughter until Tamara turned away from her, looking mildly repentant.

"They aren't cooking up anything," David insisted. "Solomon and Larissa have been trying to help me hold on to the inheritance I plan to leave to you all."

"All," Adam spat, as if the word was the most hateful thing he'd ever heard.

Solomon glanced at his half brother. He was tempted strike back, but the truth was, he understood the man. If the shoe had been on the other foot, he didn't know how he would feel if his mother introduced a long-lost sibling and then told him that he would be splitting his inheritance with this stranger. But Solomon's mother wasn't handing out checks, because she didn't have money like David Davison. So, Solomon would never know just how awful Adam felt about the situation. But if Adam kept up with his attitude, Solomon was going to give him something else he could feel.

Alma picked up the tray of snacks that she and Larissa had prepared and began passing it around the room. "Everybody fill your plate," she said. "Then let's pray and figure out what's going on."

CHAPTER 8

Solomon knew what was going on. His client's case was being sabotaged. After meeting with Lamar and hearing all the information he had gathered, Solomon was more convinced than ever that one, if not more, of David's kids was involved. But what he couldn't figure out was why one of his children would want to embarrass his or her father in such a manner.

Regardless, he wasn't going to stand by and let them destroy his client. He was now seated in the office of the court reporter, waiting on Summer Jones and her attorney to arrive for the scheduled deposition, during which Solomon hoped to figure out which of David's kids were involved.

As the court reporter set up her equipment in the conference room, Solomon received a text message. He looked down at his phone and saw that it was Larissa.

Are we still on for lunch?

He responded, **Yes, how does Nana's Uptown sound to you?**

She wrote back, **Perfect. I'll meet you at the courthouse, and we can walk over there.**

Meet me at noon. After typing those words, Solomon put his phone down and stood up to greet his "deponent" as she walked in with her attorney. Solomon held out his hand. "Ms. Summer Jones, I presume?" He extended a hand. "I'm Solomon Harris."

"I know," she said as she shook his hand, then released it like a dirty napkin.

"Harold Stiles," said the man with her, shaking Solomon's hand. "Summer's attorney."

Solomon nodded. "Glad that you could join us today." He indicated the court reporter. "This is Patricia Miller-Harding. She'll be recording our conversation today. Because this lawsuit has the potential of running into the millions, we are doing an audiovisual recording while Patricia takes notes."

Summer's chin jutted out. "I'm tired of these preachers getting away with their messes, so you can film me all day long. I don't care."

Her attorney put a hand on her arm, already trying to rein his client in. Solomon smiled. He could tell that this was going to be good. "How about you, Mr. Stiles?" he said. "Any objection to the recording devices?"

Stiles sat down. "You're within your rights to use them. As you said, this lawsuit may draw out to the millions."

Solomon took a sip of his water. He then turned to the deponent and said, "State your name for the record, please."

After Summer stated her name, the others in the room did the same.

Solomon searched through his notes as if he didn't have all of the questions he needed to ask in his head. "The plaintiff's name is Winter Sawyer. Is she your daughter?"

"Yes."

"How old is she?"

"Fourteen. Oh, but she was thirteen at the time she was being counseled by Pastor Davison."

Summer's attorney nodded, as if he'd instructed her to mention the girl's age. That was alright, because Solomon wanted the information brought out, as well. But he'd get back to that later. "Where do you work, Ms. Jones?" he asked next.

"At a grocery store on the west side of town."

"And how much do you earn a year?"

"What do my client's annual earnings have to do with anything?" Stiles asked.

Looking at his notes again, Solomon prepared to let them have it. He normally would have saved this kind of information for the trial, but his client did not want the case to see the inside of a courtroom. He put his notepad down and looked at Stiles. "Our investigation uncovered the fact that Ms. Jones recently deposited ten thousand dollars. Now, where does a woman who earns roughly fifteen thousand a year get her hands on a lump sum of ten grand?"

"If you knew how much I earn, why'd you bother to ask?" Summer said, sounding grumpy.

"Just how did your investigator get Ms. Jones's banking account information?" Stiles demanded.

Solomon shrugged. "I try not to ask our investigator too many questions. But if we go to court, you had best believe that Ms. Jones will have to answer questions about it. Is she prepared to do that?"

"Ain't nobody's business what's in my bank account," Summer said. But her voice faltered slightly, and she looked nervous.

"But can you explain it? Where did the money come from, Ms. Jones?" Solomon leaned closer to her as he said, "Because a jury will find that deposit very curious."

"What are you trying to say?" Stiles piped up.

"You know what I'm getting at," Solomon told him. "I think you need to talk to your client and discover if she really wants to take this to court."

"Of course I want to take this to court." Summer started doing the neck roll. "That preacher messed with my baby. He gonna pay for that."

"That's the other thing I'd like to ask you about." Solomon shuffled back through his notes. "When you arrived, you stated that you were 'tired of these preachers getting away with their messes.'"

"Yeah, and…?" Summer's attitude was on full display.

"You also referred to the plaintiff as your 'baby,' correct?"

Summer nodded. "She's my last born, so she's my baby."

"Then why would you, being the concerned mother that you are, leave your baby alone with a preacher when you have such low opinions of them?"

"I never said I had a low opinion of preachers."

"Your words indicate that you are well aware of preachers and their 'messes.' So, I'll ask you again: Why on earth would you leave your daughter in the hands of someone you thought might harm her?"

"I never thought Pastor Davison would do anything to Winter," Summer said. "And anyway, I couldn't be at those counseling sessions because I had to work."

Solomon smiled. "Our records indicate that you were laid off from work at the time of your daughter's counseling sessions. So, where were you working? Hopefully, you'll be able to report your earnings to the IRS."

"That's enough, Mr. Harris," Stiles put in. "We get your point."

Solomon took a deep breath, then leveled Summer with a steady gaze. "Are you aware that at each and every one of your daughter's counseling sessions with Pastor David Davison, Dr. Larissa Wilkinson was present? And that your daughter was not, at any time, alone with either one of them?"

"That's what he claims," Summer said.

"Can you prove he's lying? You never attended any of the sessions," Solomon reminded her.

"You're just trying to twist and turn things. I believe my daughter." Summer jumped out of her seat. "I'm getting out of here."

"Talk to your daughter again, Ms. Jones," Solomon said as she stormed out of the conference room. "Make sure this is a fight you are prepared to have. I wouldn't want anyone to perjure herself."

Stiles stood and nodded at Solomon. "I'll be in touch."

"My client does not want these false allegations to continue," Solomon told him. "We would like to settle this matter as soon as possible. So, talk with your client and see what she really wants."

"I'll get back with you," Stiles said before exiting the room.

As the court reporter stopped typing, Solomon thanked her and then checked his watch. He was about to take a very lovely lady out to lunch, but he needed to make a quick phone call first.

He pulled out his cell phone and pressed Lamar's number. When he answered, Solomon said, "How was the flight?"

"I made it home, so I'm not complaining."

"That bad, huh?"

"It was bumpy. But I tried not to let it traumatize me."

Laughing, Solomon said, "I won't keep you long; I just called to let you know that your report on Summer Jones came in handy. She'll be thinking twice about taking this case to court."

"Glad I could help. I'll see you when you get back to LA."

"Alright. See you soon."

Walking out of the courthouse, Solomon thought about going to the garage to pick up his car, but then he remembered that Larissa said they could walk over to the restaurant from here. He saw Larissa walking down the street. Solomon lifted a hand letting her know that he saw her as he stepped into the street to meet her.

Smiling, Solomon was oblivious to his surroundings; he saw only Larissa. But then he heard the screeching of tires and turned toward the noise just in time to see the car barreling in his direction. Solomon jumped to get out of the way, but the car swerved with him. Everything happened so fast. The next thing he knew, he'd leaped into the bushes behind a barrier wall in front of the courthouse. And then there was impact.

"Solomon!" Larissa screamed as she rushed over to him. "Are you okay?"

"You're the doctor. You tell me," Solomon said. He tried to stand but ended up falling back down.

"Don't move. I'm calling for an ambulance."

Solomon glanced at the angel standing above him. He tried to speak, but his mouth wouldn't open, and he began drifting into darkness.

CHAPTER 9

*W*hat happened, ma'am?"

"I don't know. Everything happened so fast. It looked like the car was chasing him, but that can't be right." Larissa was beside herself with worry as she stood in the hospital waiting room answering the police officer's questions.

"Does he have any enemies that you know of?" the officer asked.

"No, Solomon doesn't have any enemies here. He doesn't even live here. He's been visiting family." Then Larissa thought of her cousins and how much contempt they held for Solomon. She wished she had been able to see the driver of that car, if only to console herself with the knowledge that no one in their family had been responsible for running him down. She turned back to the officer. "I don't have any answers.

You'll have to get those from Solomon, and I really need to get back there to see if he is okay."

"Good idea. Maybe he recognized the driver of that runaway car." The officer pointed toward the emergency room doors. "You lead the way."

Breathing a sigh of relief, Larissa hit the button to open the emergency room doors, then walked through the double doors and up to the nurses' station. Since she worked there, she counted on the hospital personnel being up-front and honest with her. "Hey, Erin," she said, catching the attention of one of the nurses behind the counter. "I'm looking for a patient. I forgot to ask the room number."

"Not a problem," Erin said. She sat at a computer and started clicking. "Patient's name?"

"Solomon Harris."

"Oh, I don't have to look him up. He's mine." Erin pointed down the hall. "Bed twelve."

"How's he doing?"

"A little banged up…bruised ribs and a sprained arm. He'll be in a lot of pain for a few days, but he'll live."

"Thanks, Erin." Larissa headed for Solomon's room with the officer following behind. She had wanted to go into Solomon's room when they had arrived at the hospital, but she knew all too well how family and friends sometimes got in the way during the most critical times of patient care. So, she'd opted to hang back and wait for the police officer to arrive.

But now she was anxious to get to his room. As she pulled back the curtain, Larissa flinched as she heard Solomon yell out in pain. She rushed to his side. "Are you okay? What hurts?"

Solomon looked up at her and smiled. "I didn't know that you were here."

"I rode with you in the ambulance. You were still a little out of it when they rolled you back here."

"That was you standing over me after that maniac tried to run me down?"

"Of course it was me. I told you that I was calling an ambulance. Do you remember that?"

"I thought you were an angel. You look so much like one, I see how I got mixed up."

Larissa giggled. "You can't stop flirting even while you're in a hospital bed suffering with pain, can you?"

"Never," Solomon told her.

The police officer stepped forward then, so Larissa told Solomon, "Officer Walker is here to talk to you. Do you think you're up to answering his questions?"

Solomon nodded, and the questions began.

"Did you see the person who tried to hit you, Mr. Harris?" the officer asked him.

"I looked right at her. It was Summer Jones."

Larissa gasped.

"And how do you know this woman?"

"I just finished deposing her for an upcoming trial." Solomon shrugged a shoulder. "I guess she didn't like my line of questioning."

"That's terrible!" Larissa finally managed. "I had no idea Summer was so violent, or I never would have asked you to take this case. Solomon, you've got to believe me." She was close to tears.

"It's not your fault, Larissa. I'm not going to let you blame yourself for this."

"Then who should we blame?" Leah asked, whisking into the room. "Because Larissa had no business getting you mixed up in this."

Surprise came over Solomon as he looked at his half sister. "What are you doing here?"

"I came to get you. Mama and Daddy don't want you going back to your hotel, and they made me promise to bring you to them."

"I'm fine. I don't need any babysitters."

"Daddy hasn't been able to rest since he heard about your accident. He's agitated and overcome with worry right now."

"Just tell him that I'm okay. There's no need for me to spend the night in his house to prove that I'm still alive."

Leah put her hands on her hips. "I'm not taking no for an answer, so if you don't come with me, this police officer will have to arrest me for stalking you. Because I'll be moving into your hotel room."

The police officer glanced at Leah, then looked to Solomon. "Please don't make me arrest her."

Larissa touched Solomon's arm. "It's the right move, Solomon. With your ribs and your wrist the way they are, you're going to need help. We can all look after you if you come stay at Uncle David's."

Having Larissa in close proximity was an idea that Solomon could get with. Suddenly, being in his father's house didn't seem like the worst thing in the world. "Alright, fine. Leah, I'll go with you. But someone will have to pick up my car from the parking garage and gather my things from the hotel."

"Leah and I will take care of that," Larissa told him. "You just need to get some rest once the doctor releases you."

"My work here is done," the police officer said. "I'll give you a call once we have something on your case."

"Thanks," Solomon said.

Nurse Erin entered the room and asked everyone to step outside so she could bandage his ribs and arm.

Leah and Larissa quickly moved out of the nurse's way. They went back into the waiting area and sat down with each other. Larissa's mind was going a mile a minute trying to figure out why Leah had even bothered showing up at the hospital. She had made it perfectly clear how she felt about Solomon. But Larissa would do her best not to judge her cousin's act of kindness.

"You don't think I should be here, do you?" Leah said, bursting into Larissa's thoughts.

Larissa blinked. "You're his family, too. If you want to be here, you should. I'm just a bit confused as to *why* you want to."

"I'm not evil, you know," Leah insisted. "I may not be happy about the fact that I have a half brother, but I would never want to see him hurt."

"I don't think you're an evil person," Larissa said gently. "You do tend to hold grudges, but I wouldn't call you evil."

"Gee, thanks. With that vote of confidence, I probably should be running for dogcatcher."

"I didn't mean it like that. Even though you resented it, you and I were raised like sisters, and I love you." Larissa leaned over and gave Leah a hug.

Leah patted her on the back. "I know I'm not the easiest person to get along with, but I love you, too. And if I haven't told you before, I'm very proud of all you've managed to accomplish."

Larissa knew the part that Leah didn't say but was thinking: "*even though you had two screwups for parents.*" But Larissa would take a compliment from Leah in whatever form it came. "Thanks, girl. I appreciate that." She stood up. "Let's get back to Solomon's room so we can see when they plan to release him."

"You really like him, don't you?" Leah asked as she stood and followed Larissa.

"He's not so bad...and he's practically family."

"You know that's not what I mean." Leah gave her a nudge. "He's not really your cousin, you know."

"Whatever." Larissa walked through the double doors, shaking her head at her cousin's comment. But, in truth, she was beginning to wonder if her feelings for Solomon were turning into something more.

⌦⌫⌦

The hospital was planning on keeping Solomon overnight for observation, but they agreed to his release when Larissa assured them that she would look after him.

Solomon grinned. "Aw, isn't that sweet? See, I knew you cared about me."

Larissa turned a mock glare on him. "Shut up, bonehead, or I'll let them keep you here for a week. Have you ever eaten hospital food?"

Solomon made a gesture of locking his lips shut. He received his release paperwork in about an hour and then left the hospital with Larissa and Leah.

Once they arrived at the house, Leah practically ran over Larissa in her attempts to see to Solomon's comfort.

"What's gotten into you?" Solomon asked his half sister. "You don't like me, remember?"

"No matter how I feel about you, I would never want to see you hurt. All I'm trying to do is make you more comfortable. If you don't want my help, I'll just go get Larissa. You like her better anyway."

If he wasn't already banged and bruised up, Solomon would have kicked himself. Leah was just trying to help him, and he was making her feel unwelcome simply because he wanted Larissa in his room. "Sorry. That's not what I meant," he said. "Thank you for all you've done to make me a little more comfortable."

Smiling, Leah waved a pill bottle in his face. "I brought something else that might make you feel better."

"Are those my pain meds?"

"Sure are. Larissa thought you might be needing them by now."

"She thought right. I was hoping that this pain in my ribs would go away, but it hasn't gone anywhere. If anything, it's gotten worse."

Leah handed him a glass of water and two pills. "Take these. If the pain doesn't subside, let one of us know, and we'll put a call in to the doctor to see if you can get a stronger dosage."

"Thanks, Leah." Solomon swallowed the pills, then lay back against his pillow and waited for the medicine to do its job. As he began feeling the effects, he wondered why Leah had suddenly decided to be nice to him.

⌖

"How dare you call me for help!" Leah screamed into the phone. "I'm glad the police are looking for you."

"Why are you being like this, Leah?" Summer asked. "I thought we had a deal."

"I certainly never asked you to run Solomon down. What kind of crazy person does something like that?"

"He's on to us, Leah. He knows that someone gave me ten thousand dollars right around the time that I filed the claim against your father."

"So what? You don't try to kill someone because your get-rich-quick scheme goes bust."

"You don't understand. I was counting on that money to finally get out of this godforsaken apartment."

Leah wanted to scream at the woman and tell her that Solomon was her half brother—that, no matter how upset she had been with her father when she'd learned of his long-kept secret, she would never even consider physically hurting her own flesh and blood. But she'd done that already, hadn't she, when her scheme to get back at her father had back-fired with him having a heart attack?

Leah realized that it was time for her to bite the bullet and con-fess all her misdeeds to her family. But before she would do that, Leah thought that this was a good time to pray. She got down on her knees and bowed her head. "Dear Lord, I'm so sorry for what I've done. I don't know what I was thinking, only that I became so angry when I discov-ered what dad had been doing. I know Your Word tells us that it is okay to be angry, but our anger should not cause us to sin. And my anger has fueled everything I've done lately, so I know that I have sinned against You, Lord, and against my dad. Help me, Lord. Take the anger out of my heart and forgive me. And help my family to forgive me for what I have done. Thank You for loving me, God, even though I've made a ter-rible mistake. Amen."

Getting off her knees, Leah straightened her posture and went downstairs to talk to her parents.

CHAPTER 10

W ell, our patient is finally resting," Larissa told her aunt and uncle as she entered the family room.

"Good. I've been worried about that boy all day long," David said.

"Leah told you that she was going to sit with him at the hospital, so you should have stopped all that worrying," Alma admonished him. "You know it isn't good for your heart."

"I'm just thankful that Larissa and Leah were there to watch over him."

"I didn't do much, Uncle David, but you should have seen Leah," Larissa said. "She practically threatened to get herself arrested if Solomon didn't agree to come back to the house with us."

David smiled. "That's my girl."

But Alma wasn't smiling as she said, "I just don't understand why that woman would say such awful things about you, and then try to kill Solomon for just doing his job as our attorney. She must have some mental issues."

"She didn't seem crazy to me," David said, shaking his head. "That's why I can't explain it. If I'd known something like this would happen, I never would have pressured Solomon into taking this case."

"I don't think any of us will understand a person like Summer Jones," Larissa told him. "But I can tell you this: Nothing Summer did was your fault, Uncle David, so you should stop feeling guilty about it. Solomon will recover from his injuries, and Summer will pay for what she's done to this family."

Leah came into the room and sat down in a chair across from her mother and father. She put her hands over her stomach and leaned forward, biting her lip.

"Is something wrong, honey?" David asked her. "You look so sad."

"I have to tell you something, Daddy, and I'm just worried that you're going to hate me after I tell you what I've done."

David sat up. "I could never hate my own flesh and blood. Why would you even think a thing like that?"

Tears were streaming down Leah's face as she said, "I did it. I paid Summer to accuse you of molesting her daughter." After blurting out those words, Leah's tears became a waterfall. "I'm so sorry. I'm so, so sorry for what I've done."

Other than Leah's crying, the room was silent for several beats before Alma said, "Why would you do a thing like that?"

Leah lowered her head. "As Daddy's public relations manager, I have full access to his files at church. One day, I found a file marked 'Solomon Harris.' I wasn't familiar with the name, and I was curious." She started crying again, then looked up at her father. "You should have told us, Daddy. You and Mama had no right to keep that from us."

"I'm sorry that I let you down, Leah."

The moment those words were out of David's mouth, Alma stood up, outraged. "Why in the world are you apologizing to her?" She turned to Leah. "Do you know what you've done? My husband almost died over that woman's allegations, and to discover that my own child had something to do with it…" Alma's voice caught as she started hyperventilating.

"Calm down, Alma," David said, his voice steady, gentle. "No sense in you having a heart attack and joining me on this sickbed."

"Please sit down, Aunt Alma," Larissa echoed. "Uncle David's right—you're getting way too worked up." She turned to Leah. "Can you just explain to everyone why you thought having this woman extort money from Uncle David was a good idea?"

"I'm sorry, Mama."

"You're sorry. Is that all you have to say for yourself?" Alma took a few deep breaths as she tried to calm herself.

"I was just so mad," Leah responded, but as her mother started to get up again, she quickly added, "But I may have overreacted."

"Even if discovering that you had a brother upset you, I don't see the need for extortion." Larissa stared at her, completely confused.

"This is a lot to take in right now. Can you help us understand what you were thinking?" David still spoke in a calm, even voice.

Leah pointed at Larissa. "Larissa and I are the same age. When it came time for me to go to college, you and Mama sat me down and told me that there wasn't enough money in the college fund for me to go to UCLA, my preferred college, and I accepted that because I knew that Adam was in college at that time, and that you would be footing the bill for Larissa's college expenses, as well."

"Your mother and I tried our best to save as much as we could for college, but we weren't earning as much in those days as we do now," David tried to explain.

"Then how come Solomon was able to go to Harvard?" Leah demanded. "Why wasn't he told to scale back on his college dreams and be a good little team player like I was?"

"Your father had no say in Solomon's decision to go to Harvard, or any other school he might have chosen, for that matter," Alma said.

"I think you're allowing yourself to be deceived, Mama. Daddy practically has a siren to Solomon in that folder of his. And I'm willing to bet that you've never seen any of its contents."

Alma looked from her daughter to her husband. "What is she talking about, David?"

Sighing, David turned to Larissa. "Would you mind going to my office and getting that file on your way home from work tomorrow?"

"Mama doesn't have to wait another day," Leah piped up. "I can go get that file tonight and bring it back."

"No, you've done enough," Alma said. "I'll look at it tomorrow." With that said, Alma got up and started for the door. Before leaving the room, she turned back to Leah and said, "I'd start looking for a new job if I were you. Because I'm going to begin looking for a new public relations manager for the church first thing tomorrow."

Leah leaped out of her chair. "You can't fire me. I work for Dad and the church, not you."

"Your father is in no position to run that church, thanks to you and that woman you hired to spew all types of false allegations at him." Alma huffed, then took a deep breath and said, "Please clean out your desk. We'll give you two months' severance pay. That should give you enough time to find another job." With that, she left the room.

"Are you really going to let her do this to me, Daddy?" Leah pouted. "Where am I supposed to find another job on such short notice?"

David held out his arms. "Come here, Leah." When she stepped into his embrace, David hugged her, then told her, "Things will work out. Just give me some time to talk to your mother."

Pulling out of his arms, Leah asked, "Why do you have to talk to her about this? Why can't you just tell her to stay out of it? How can she just fire me like that?"

Larissa couldn't take any more of Leah's pity party. She knew she should stay out of it and just let Uncle David handle his daughter, but he was trying to recover from his own ailments and didn't need Leah's drama. "What you did was wrong, Leah," Larissa said before she could stop herself. "Aunt Alma had every right to fire you."

Leah swung around, becoming hysterical. "You stay out of this, Larissa. All you've ever done is try to steal my father's affections from me. And now that I've admitted what I did, you just want to make yourself look good in Daddy's eyes. But he's not your father, and you need to remember that."

"He may not be my father, but he's the closest thing to a father that I've ever known."

David lifted a hand. "I'm not going to have the two of you arguing like you used to when you were kids. I thought this dispute had been settled a long time ago." He turned to Leah. "Your mother and I adopted Larissa when it was clear that her parents weren't coming back for her, so she is as much my daughter as you and Tamara. I hope we are done with this conversation once and for all."

"You have always preferred Larissa over me!" Leah fumed. "And now that you have your precious Solomon home, where you've wanted him all along"—she pointed in the direction of the second floor—"there's no place here for me at all."

"Leah, Leah." David shook his head. "I love you. Why do you act as if the world is against you or as if you had such a terrible childhood? Your mother and I worked hard to make sure that you had everything you needed, and we provided a lot of your wants and just-had-to-haves, too." David started to stand but then fell back onto the couch and grabbed his chest.

Larissa ran to her uncle and unbuttoned the top button of his pajama shirt. "Can you breathe? Where does it hurt?"

"What's wrong with him?" Leah asked, looking petrified.

"Go get Aunt Alma," Larissa screamed.

"I'm okay," David said. "Just give me a minute." He tried to sit up, but then he quickly lay back down again.

When Alma ran into the room, Larissa said, "Get me an aspirin."

"Oh my Lord, God in heaven, please Jesus, help my husband." Alma left the room in a state of panic but quickly returned with the aspirin and a glass of water. As Larissa gave David the aspirin, Alma's composure seemed to return to her. "Don't just stand there," she said to Leah. "Call for an ambulance."

As Leah headed for the phone, Solomon stumbled into the room. "W-what...what's going on?" he asked, just before falling on the ground and knocking himself unconscious.

"Tell them we need two beds on that ambulance!" Alma hollered to Leah.

Chapter 11

oth David and Solomon were required to spend the night in the hospital for observation. When they came back home the next day, Alma had two makeshift beds set up in the family room. She wanted to be able to watch both of them, to make sure neither man got up or did anything he wasn't supposed to do for the next forty-eight hours. She also wanted to make sure that her children didn't inadvertently say something that would upset her husband. When they were settled, she told them, "Consider me your warden, boys, because I'm going to guard the both of you like you've been indicted for bad health and sentenced to bed rest. Do we understand each other?"

"Better just go on and agree with her," David said to Solomon. "I know this woman, and I can tell you that she's not going to let us out of her sight."

"She shouldn't let you out of her sight—you've got the heart problem," Solomon retorted. "But I'm good."

Larissa groaned. "You had a concussion, Solomon. You need just as much rest as Uncle David, and I plan to help Aunt Alma guard her prisoners."

"Traitor," Solomon shot back. But he was smiling at her like a boy smiles at a girl when he's feeling something for her.

Larissa stared right back at him, eyes glazing over with emotions that she couldn't comprehend or explain.

David cleared his throat. "Did you bring the box that I asked you to pick up?"

As if snapping out of a trance, Larissa jerked and then turned to her uncle. "Of course I did. I swung by the church before coming here to check on you and Solomon. You know I got your back."

"You always have, and I'm so thankful that I was allowed to raise you," David said to her.

Seated on the sofa across the room, Leah and Tamara exchanged glances, and then Leah whispered something to her sister.

Larissa ignored them and put her hand on David's shoulder. "And I'm thankful for you, too, but you already know that." She smiled. "Let me run out to my car. I'll be right back with the box."

Leah popped up out of her seat and went to her father. "You don't have to do this, Daddy. I had no right going in through your file cabinet in the first place. I feel bad enough about what I've done to you and Solomon. So, let's just forget about that file. Okay?"

"Well, now I'm even more interested in the box that you said my husband was hiding from me," Alma said, sitting down next to David.

She looked him in the eye. "I've trusted you with my life and my heart for over thirty years now. Please tell me that there's nothing in that box that's going to change that."

"No, baby, I've never been unfaithful to you since the time when we were separated." He turned away and quietly added, "But I have kept in contact with Sheila over the years."

Solomon's head swiveled around. "You kept in contact with my mother? For what reason?"

"Not for what you're thinking," David said.

Larissa tried to contain her curiosity as she went to her car and retrieved the box. She carried it inside and placed it on Alma's lap.

"Open it," David told his wife.

She shook her head, then stood up and handed the box to Solomon. "I don't want to open it. I'm afraid of what I'll find." Taking a deep breath, Alma patted her chest and concentrated on calming herself.

Tamara glared at Leah. "See what you stirred up?" She got up and came to stand next to her mother.

David reached for his wife's hand. She held on to him as he said, "I did everything I could so that I wouldn't hurt you again, Alma. And I never complained about not being able to have Solomon in my life…but I had to know how he was doing. I couldn't live with just sending money and not knowing what he was up to. You understand that, don't you?"

Alma remained silent.

Solomon opened the box and began taking out photo after photo, arranging them across the blanket spread over his lap. Larissa picked up one of the pictures and showed it to Solomon. "You said 'cheese' like that with your two front teeth missing?"

Solomon grinned. "That was from first grade. I had just lost my two front teeth, but my mom convinced me that I was just as handsome without them."

Tamara grabbed the picture from Larissa and laughed. "Your mama lied to you."

Solomon ignored her comment as he pulled out another picture. "Here I am playing football in high school." He squinted at the photo, his brow furrowed in confusion. "Was this taken from the bleachers?"

"Yep," David answered.

"My mom never sat that far up in the bleachers. She wouldn't have been able to get this angle with her camera."

"Let me see that," Alma said, taking the picture from Solomon. She studied it, then flipped it over as if to check for a date. Then she turned to David with a look of comprehension. "So that's why you accepted that speaking engagement in California four years in a row, even though they couldn't afford to pay you the normal rate."

David shrugged. "I preached there for free. You got a mini vacation out of it," he reminded her.

"Mmph. I was out shopping and going to the spa...the one you made sure I had a gift certificate for every time I traveled to California with you. I always felt guilty for leaving you all alone. Meanwhile, you were out spying on Solomon."

"Did my mom know that you were there?" Solomon asked.

David shook his head. "She knew that I attended one of your games each year, but I never told her when I was coming. I didn't want to break my promise to Alma about not seeing Sheila ever again."

"She sent you a copy of my diploma and my bachelor's degree certificate." Solomon pulled the items out of the box with a mystified look on his face.

"From what I've been told," Tamara chimed in, "Daddy paid a lot of money for your education. The least your mother could have done was send him proof of your graduations, don't you think?"

Solomon didn't respond. He was speechless.

"I'm so sorry, David," Alma murmured. "I just don't know how you put up with me all these years." Her eyes brimmed with tears as she stood and ran from the room.

"Go get your mama and bring her back here to me," David said to Leah.

Leah shook her head. "I'm the last one she wants to see right now. Send Tamara. Or Larissa."

"Why is she so upset, Daddy?" Tamara asked.

"I don't know. Just bring her back to me."

"It's okay," Larissa said. "I'll go."

<hr />

While Larissa went to summon her aunt, Solomon continued looking at the contents of the box. Leah walked over to him. "I'm so sorry for everything I did and especially that you were injured as a result of my anger," she said quietly. "But now that you're looking at Daddy's shrine to you, can you at least begin to understand why I was so upset?"

"I can understand," Solomon told her. "And I'm not angry with you about my injuries. You didn't tell that woman to try to run me over with her car."

"I know, but if I hadn't gotten Summer involved in our family matters, this never would have happened to you.

Solomon smiled at another photo of him. "Forget about it, Leah," he said. "We're family, right?"

Leah hesitated a moment, looked at her father, then turned back to Solomon, nodding her head. "Right. We're family."

<hr />

"Aunt Alma, Uncle David's worried about you," Larissa told her aunt when she'd found her in her bedroom. "He wants you to come back to the family room and be with us."

"I can't go back in there." Alma shook her head. "I just can't face him."

"You can't face who? Solomon?"

Alma plopped down on her bed. She put her head in her hand and massaged her forehead. "Either one of them…your uncle or Solomon."

"What's wrong, Aunt Alma? You're supposed to be the warden of this hold-them-down-and-make-sure-they-don't-get-up operation, remember? If you don't come back down there, who's going to guard them?"

"Maybe I'm the one who should be on lockdown," Alma said with a sigh. "Somebody should come and arrest me for denying Solomon the right to have a father in his life all these years. And look what I reduced my husband to…sneaking around, snapping pictures from a distance."

"Uncle David could have divorced you if he wanted to be with Solomon's mother. You don't have anything to worry about."

"I'm not worried about Sheila. Your uncle and I were young, dumb, and godless back then. But once we made up our minds that we wanted our marriage to last and committed to let God lead us, I've never had a reason to doubt him, not even once."

"Then why are you so upset now?" Larissa sat down next to her aunt and started rubbing her back.

"Do you remember how your uncle was with you and your cousins when you were kids?"

Larissa smiled, conjuring images of her happy childhood in her god-parents' home. "Uncle David always made time for each of us. When I think back to those days, I sometimes wonder how he knew just how to make each of us feel so special. We took it for granted, though…

especially Leah. She always seemed to feel as if someone else was getting more of this or that than she was."

"Leah is more like me than I realized," Alma said, her voice heavy with regret.

"What do you mean?"

"I kept your uncle away from Solomon because my biggest fear was that he might love him more than he loved the children we had together. I now realize how foolish that was. David has more than enough love to go around, and the proof was the way he doted equally on our children and on you, Larissa. He's always loved you like you were his own daughter, but he didn't play favorites." Tears rolled down Alma's face. "I don't deserve that man. I can only pray that he will forgive me for what I did to him."

"You're being too hard on yourself, Aunt Alma. Uncle David isn't entirely innocent. You two weren't divorced but only separated when he took up with Solomon's mother. If a husband of mine did me wrong like that, he probably would have received a divorce petition long ago."

Wiping her face, Alma admitted, "I held the threat of divorce papers over David's head for at least three years after we got back together. He just kept proving to me that he was a changed man. I eventually fell more in love with him than I had been when we first got married. But his love for me has cost him a great deal, and I need to find a way to make that up to him."

"I don't think Uncle David is keeping count of who owes what," Larissa said. "Just come back to the family room and sit with him. That's all he wants right now."

Alma patted her daughter's leg as she stood up with a look of resignation on her face. "If I don't know anything else, I know that my husband loves and honors me. It's time for me to start honoring him."

CHAPTER 12

*W*here do you think you're going?" Portia asked Adam as he put on his jacket and grabbed his car keys.

"To my parents' house. I need to check on my dad."

"Can't you just call him? You've been so busy that we've hardly had anytime to discuss our strategy."

"What strategy?" Adam asked.

Portia rose from the seat at her vanity in their master suite and rubbed lotion on her hands as she sauntered over to him, her floor-length gown billowing as she walked. "Don't play games with me, Adam. I didn't sign up to be a wife to an associate pastor all my life. You promised me big things, and now's our chance to get everything we deserve."

Adam pressed a hand to his temple. "Portia, I don't think that you understand how things work."

Moving away from him, Portia flung over her shoulder, "Don't talk down to me. I know plenty. It's you who needs to catch up."

"There's no reason for you to get upset." Adam followed his wife out of their bedroom and down the stairs. "I'm just trying to get you to understand that my father is going to be the senior pastor until he retires. I will get my chance; we just have to wait a little while longer."

"I'm sick of waiting." Portia lifted her hands and pointed several different directions, indicating her spacious three-thousand-square-foot home. "All of my friends have much bigger houses than we have. They drive better cars."

"What's wrong with your brand-new Lexus?"

"It's not a Mercedes, that's what's wrong with it." Portia's hands were on her hips as her neck rolled, displaying all the attitude she possessed. "I have done my part, Adam. I gave you two beautiful children, and I did it in the right order: a son first, Micah, and then his sister, Angel. I keep your home in a fashion befitting a king. But are you grateful for anything that I do?"

"I'm grateful, Portia," Adam assured her. "I appreciate everything you do with the kids and how homey you've made our house."

"A house that I don't even like," she reminded him.

"What do you want from me, Portia? I don't know what else I can do to make you happy."

"You can take your rightful place and stand up and be the king you're meant to be, instead of humbly accepting the crumbs as they fall off your father's table."

"I'm doing the best I can," Adam managed. "I make a good living. Our children are well taken care of. All of our needs are met."

"I don't have that big house on the hill that your mother has."

"She didn't have it, either, when she was your age. My father didn't start coming into any real money until he was well into his forties."

Portia folded her arms across her chest and told him flat out, "I'm not waiting another ten years for you to become the man you should already be."

Getting agitated, Adams barked, "What do you want me to do, build my own church? Where would you suggest I build it, since this seems to be such an emergency?"

Portia scowled. "I'm not asking you to build anything except another house for me. The perfect opportunity has landed in our lap, and I just don't want you to squander it."

"What are you talking about?"

She gave him a coy smile. "That's why I was hoping you'd stay home tonight. We need to discuss our strategy."

"What strategy, Portia? I'm just keeping my head above water while my father is dealing with his illness and my illegitimate brother."

"That's what I'm talking about. Your father being temporarily indisposed gives us the perfect opportunity to tell the congregation about Solomon. Once everyone discovers that your father cheated on your mother and hid a son from everyone for all these years, getting you that senior pastor position will be a cakewalk."

"You want me to expose my father before the entire congregation?"

"Not you, necessarily...we can get someone else to do it. Maybe one of the members could stand up and shout it out during a service. Ooh, that would be good." She paced the foyer as if seeing the scene play out. "And remember, your father brought this on himself."

"Stop, Portia. This is crazy talk. I don't want anyone to know what my father has done. I couldn't care less if it would help me get some senior pastor position; this is my father we are talking about."

Portia halted her steps and planted her hands on her hips. "I don't see the problem. It's not like your father cares that we're bursting at the seams in this small house. He hasn't even given you a raise in two years."

She was right about that. But the income from tithes and offerings had declined due to the recession that had been sweeping the nation, so no one had received a raise in two years—Adam's father included. Adam had been using his credit cards more than ever before, trying to keep up with inflation and his wife's spending habits. When he'd approached his father about his financial woes, all he'd said was that Adam and Portia needed to cut back and live within their means.

But Adam couldn't do that. The beauty queen wife he'd married didn't believe in living within her means. "We'll talk when I get back," Adam told her, then headed for the door.

But Portia apparently wasn't ready to let the conversation go. As Adam opened the front door, she shouted at him, "Wake up, Adam. Your father has given away part of your inheritance. He's not being loyal to you. It's time for us to worry about our own family."

"I'll see you when I get back." Adam left the house and got in his car. He sat in the driveway for a moment, trying to get his head together, before starting the engine and backing into the street. He hadn't been raised with a gimme-gimme mind-set, as Portia had. In the early years, his parents hadn't had much, but they had taught their children the value of a roof over your head, clothes on your back, and a full stomach. All of that had spelled "love" to the Davison children.

Adam's wife and children had much more than Adam ever dreamed of having when he was a young boy, but it was never enough for Portia. Now he was expected to betray his father? He'd done enough of that already, as far as Adam was concerned. And what he was about to do would be a serious betrayal to his half brother. So, Portia would have to clear her mind of all her schemes, because Adam didn't need one more thing to repent of and seek forgiveness for.

"About time," Summer said, opening the door of her motel room to admit Adam. "I thought you'd never get here."

"I was at home with my wife when you called," he said as he entered. "I couldn't just get up and leave without talking to her first."

"You used to get up and leave whenever I called. When the two of you were just boyfriend and girlfriend, I almost convinced you to leave her and stay where you belonged." She inched her way toward him, brushed against his arm, and said, "It's not too late. You can still come back."

He stepped away from her. "I made my choice. And after what you tried to do to my father, I'm thankful that I didn't marry you."

"We all had choices to make, Adam." Summer's tone was more malicious than he'd ever heard it. "You left us as if we didn't mean a thing to you, so I had to do what I had to do to survive."

"You accused my father of molesting his own granddaughter!" Adam hadn't meant to yell, but he couldn't help himself. Summer had piqued his frustration.

Summer wasn't moved. "Thanks to you, he never knew that Winter was his granddaughter. I doubt if he even noticed the resemblance."

"You knew," Adam spat back at her. "And you knew that my father never tried anything with Summer."

"Hey, your sister paid me to say that he did."

"And you even got me in on the scheme you plotted with Leah. If I had known why you wanted my father to counsel Winter, I never would have asked him to do it."

"Oh, yeah. Blame me." Summer laughed bitterly. "But when your father told you to counsel Winter, you ran from the opportunity to have a few private moments with your own daughter. If you had just done what your father asked you to do, then none of this would have happened."

"Don't give me that," Adam grumbled. "You and Leah had this whole scam cooked up from the beginning. If I had agreed to counsel Winter, you would have found another way to extort money from my father."

"Maybe I would have told him that his granddaughter needed a new pair of shoes."

"Winter doesn't need a thing. I pay child support every month. Her needs—and her wants—should be well accounted for."

Rolling her eyes, Summer told him, "Winter and I have gotten peanuts from you, while Portia and your other children get the lion's share."

"Whatever." Adam was tired of trying to get the women in his life to be reasonable. He reached in his pocket, pulled out the cash he'd brought along, and held it out to her. "I'm giving you the money you requested, but you really should turn yourself in and plead temporary insanity or something."

Summer huffed. "And who's going to take care of Winter when they lock me up? I can't count on you; you won't even acknowledge your own daughter."

Adam didn't respond. He didn't know how.

"I need you to promise that if I get caught, you'll take your rightful place in Summer's life."

Adam closed his eyes and shook his head. "I wish things were different, but there's no way I can do that."

"I'm telling you right now that if I get arrested, I will let everyone know that you're Winter's father. And she will come to live with you."

Adam felt like the most horrid man in the world as he walked away from Summer yet again. At that moment, he knew exactly how awful his father must have felt while sending child support checks to Sheila but holding back from participating in his son's life.

CHAPTER 13

*L*arissa entered the kitchen to find Alma chopping a rainbow of colorful vegetables, evidently preparing to make a heart-healthy meal for the family. She'd been on a health kick ever since David's heart attack.

Tamara came into the kitchen shortly after. Alma looked up. "Where's Leah?" she asked.

Tamara shrugged.

"I think she went home," Larissa said.

"She was probably feeling out of place," Tamara mused, "knowing how mad you are with her, Mama."

"I have every right to be upset with Leah," Alma reasoned. "My husband wouldn't be on his sickbed now if she hadn't put that crazy woman up to doing what she did." Alma handed a bag of celery to Tamara and a bunch of carrots to Larissa. "Chop those while I put the water on to boil, will you?"

Larissa picked up a knife and began dicing carrots as Alma continued the discussion.

"I'll tell you what," Alma said, filling a pot with water. "In my day, children didn't plot revenge against their parents. We were beaten back then just for looking crossways. Kids these days are too spoiled. Accustomed to getting away with everything."

"Don't be talking about that 'spare the rod, spoil the child' stuff," Larissa said. "Because I seemed to remember getting my buns warmed more than a few times by you."

"And you got the message." Alma came back to the counter with a bowl for the vegetables. "But I obviously didn't beat that Leah enough."

"You and Daddy didn't do anything wrong when it came to raising us," Tamara told her mother. "Leah has her own issues, and only Leah can make the changes that she needs to make in order to be happy."

"What are you all talking about in here?" Adam asked as he entered the kitchen.

The women looked up, and Alma reached out to hug him. "There's my son. I wondered if you were going to come by today. Are the kids with you?"

"No," Adam said, stepping back. "They're at Portia's mother's house, but I'll bring them over as soon as they come back home."

"Good. You know how much I enjoy seeing my grandchildren."

"You'd see them a lot more if you'd just give Portia a call and set it up with her." He wagged his finger playfully at her.

"I'll give her a call," Alma said, "I just don't understand that girl. She's a lot like Leah in that way. But I'll try harder to understand her." She smiled at Adam. "Now, are you hungry? Will you be able to stay for dinner?"

Adam patted his stomach. "I'm always hungry when you're cooking, Mama. Now, if it was Tamara cooking, rather than just chopping up the vegetables, I might have to pass."

"Whatever, jerk." Tamara flung a stalk of celery at her brother.

Adam laughed. "I'm going to sit in the family room with Dad, unless there's something I can do to help."

"Nothing at all," Alma said. "He'll appreciate the visit. We'll let you know when dinner's ready."

When they had finished with the preparations, Adam set up a card table in the family room so that everyone could sit with the invalids and have dinner together. David and Solomon received their meals on trays they balanced on their laps.

"I sure do thank you all for being willing to sit in my jail cell with me," David said good-naturedly.

"Ha!" Adam licked his lips. "With this scrumptious meal, I'd say you're being treated better than any prisoner I ever heard of. This is some good eating."

Alma smiled. "Thank you, Adam. You always make me feel so good about my cooking skills."

"That's because he's always hungry, 'cause Portia doesn't cook," Tamara said with a giggle.

"But she does mind her own business," Adam shot back, giving his sister the eye.

Larissa stood up and gathered her plate. "I'm moving away from the kiddie table. The two of you haven't changed a bit." She lowered herself into the chair beside Solomon's bed and resumed eating.

"Yeah, I bet it was *terrible* sitting all the way over here with us when the man you love was three feet away," Tamara said, winking at Larissa.

Rolling her eyes, Larissa told her cousin, "I'm not even going to dignify that with a response."

Solomon put his fork down and glanced at Larissa. "Please respond. I'd love to know what's going on."

"Okay, everybody leave Larissa alone," David commanded them. "Let's all just enjoy our dinner and each other's company."

"And you'd better leave me alone, too," Larissa said, pointing at Solomon, "or I'll go find Summer and bring her over here so she can run over a leg or something."

"See? That comment alone shows how much Larissa likes Solomon," Tamara said. "She wouldn't have that crazy woman do more than run over Solomon's leg. If she truly found him annoying, she would have fantasized about Summer running him down, like she tried to do."

Larissa groaned. "I'm a doctor, Tamara. I would never 'fantasize' about people getting injured. I was just joking with Solomon."

"I will just be so thankful when that woman is arrested," Alma said. "I don't feel that David or Solomon is safe as long as she's running loose."

"That's another reason for me to get out of the South as fast as I can." Solomon said.

Strange how Larissa's heart lurched at the thought. She'd gotten used to his presence and wasn't ready to say good-bye.

Adam had kept his head down and remained quiet while they'd been discussing Summer, but as soon as his father mentioned his long-lost son's imminent departure, Adam perked up. "I didn't know you were leaving already," he said to Solomon. "Are you finished with the case?"

"As finished as I can be. I doubt if Ms. Jones will file suit against your father, since she will be getting indicted for vehicular assault the minute she turns up."

"Don't you think you should hang around here until she's found?" David asked. "You'll just have to turn around and come right back." He leaned forward, looking hopeful.

"I have a life in LA that I need to get back to," Solomon said, "but I will come back once she has been captured. Don't you worry."

"Alright, Solomon. I'm counting on that." Father and son nodded at each other, sending silent communications, letting each other know that they had entered a new dimension of their relationship. Not quite father and son, Larissa reflected, but not enemies, either.

"If you need a ride to the airport, I can carve out some time to take you," Adam offered. "It's the least I can do to thank you for all that you've done to help Dad."

"Trying to get rid of me really quick, huh?"

Adam glanced around the room. All eyes were on him. He sat back down. "I didn't mean it like that. You're on the mend; I just want to help in any way I can."

"Thanks, but I think I already have a ride." Solomon glanced in Larissa's direction.

Her heart leapt, and she smiled at him. "Sure, that's not a problem. As long as you agree to rest for one more day before we plan your flight home."

"Just hate to see me go, huh, Doc?" Solomon winked at her.

She felt herself blush and hoped he hadn't noticed. "I'm just looking out for your health."

"Mmm, sure you are," Tamara said as she took her plate to the kitchen while humming "Here Comes the Bride."

"I'm glad you talked me into staying that extra day," Solomon said to Larissa as she drove him to the airport the following afternoon. "My ribs are still a little sore, but I feel a hundred percent better today than I did yesterday."

"I'm just glad you listened to me," Larissa said.

Solomon reclined in his seat and put his hands behind his head. "Wake me when we get to the airport, okay?"

"Oh no, you don't. I'm not driving you around while you go to sleep on me."

"Sorry." Solomon blinked, struggling to keep his eyes open. "I've been sleeping so much lately that I guess I'm not used to being out and about yet."

"Good thing you're not the one flying the plane."

He chuckled. "I didn't take any painkillers, so I could fly that plane if I wanted to."

Larissa took her eyes off the road and gave Solomon a sideways glance. When the car started to drift to the side, she tightened her grip on the steering wheel and swerved back to the middle of the lane.

"Whoa." Solomon raised his eyebrows. "Maybe I'm the one who should be worried about what you've been taking. Do I need to drive myself to the airport or what?" he joked.

"Sorry," Larissa said. "You just kind of shocked me there. I didn't know you could fly a plane."

Solomon laughed, pressing a hand to his ribs. "Ooh, ooh, don't make me laugh. It hurts."

She sent him a quick scowl. "I don't know what's so funny."

"I was just picturing myself trying to fly a plane. I would probably be landing in an ocean somewhere, but it wouldn't be a smooth landing like that Captain Sully experienced. If I survived, I'd probably be carted off to jail like the captain of that cruise boat who jumped ship."

"What are you saying, Solomon? Can you fly a plane, or can't you?"

"I took a few lessons, but it didn't stick."

"Do you know why I was so shocked when you said that?"

Solomon turned to her but didn't say anything.

"Adam used to fly. He loved it but gave it up after he accepted his call into the ministry." Shaking her head, Larissa added, "I think you and Adam are more alike than I originally thought."

"I'm nothing like Adam." Solomon frowned and turned away from Larissa to stare out the passenger window.

"Don't start pouting, or I'll have to tell you how much you and Adam resemble each other when you're disgruntled."

"I'm not a liar, and I don't like being compared to men who are."

"Adam's not a liar," Larissa insisted. "He's one of the good guys. He married Portia when he was just twenty-one. He loves his family and treats them like gold. And I think he makes a decent pastor."

Solomon brought his gaze back to Larissa. "While you're singing his praises, did you ever stop to ask yourself why Adam pushed Summer and her daughter on Pastor David?"

"You mean, on your dad? You can stop calling him 'Pastor David,' you know."

"No, I'd rather not. Pastor David has never acknowledged me as his son to anyone but his immediate family. I don't think that earns him the right to be called 'Daddy' by me."

Larissa sent him a look of concern. "I thought the two of you had really started connecting."

Solomon shrugged. "He's alright. I will admit that I don't mind getting to know him. But that will take time. I have some stuff I need to figure out first."

"Fair enough," Larissa said as she pulled up to the gate at the airport.

Just before getting out of the car, Solomon leaned over, put his arms around Larissa, and pressed his lips against hers, all the while silently praying that she wouldn't recoil from him.

To his relief, Larissa held on to him and kissed him right back. When they finally broke apart, she was panting, and her face was flushed. "What was that for?"

"Just letting you know how much I'm going to miss you."

"Point taken." Larissa popped the trunk and got out of the car on wobbly legs. She held on to the door handle, steadying herself as she took a deep breath.

"The kiss was that good, huh?" Solomon toyed with her as he stood on the other side of the car with his hands on the hood, staring at her with star-struck eyes.

"Don't flatter yourself," Larissa told him with a smile. "We've just been driving too long. My legs needed to adjust."

"Yeah, that forty-minute drive was a real killer."

"Shut up," she said as she pulled his suitcase out of the trunk.

Solomon took the suitcase from Larissa, then hugged her and gave her a quick peck on the cheek. "I meant what I said. I'm going to miss you."

She nodded. "I'll miss you, too.

"Thanks for the ride." Solomon headed for the door, then turned back and said, "Keep in mind what I said about Adam. I don't trust him, and neither should you."

CHAPTER 14

"What are you doing?" Adam asked Leah when he found her packing boxes in her office at the church.

"Didn't you hear?" Leah asked without looking up. "Mama fired me."

Adam leaned against the doorjamb. "I know she said that, but she'll get over it. Just leave your stuff here and take a two-week vacation or something."

Leah turned to him then with sorrow in her eyes. "I think you'd better start looking for another public relations specialist. Mama is calling the shots right now, and she doesn't trust me to handle any church business."

Adam hesitated, unsure if he should ask, but then went for it. "What made you do it?"

"I don't know. Just being stupid, I guess." She turned to the wall, removed a framed award she'd received for her dedication to the ministry, and lowered it into the box. "I was angry at Dad, but I feel terrible that he ended up getting ill over all of this."

"You didn't mean for Daddy to have a heart attack," Adam told her. "Everybody makes mistakes, you know. Don't be so hard on yourself."

"If I was as *perfect* as you and Tamara, maybe I wouldn't be so hard on myself." Leah picked up her box and brushed past him out of the office.

As Adam watched his sister walk away, looking so dejected, he wished he could tell her just how imperfect he really was. But, in a way, he was even more upset with Leah than his mother was. If Leah hadn't gone and dug up her old high-school buddy, he wouldn't need to worry that his sins were about to be revealed.

Adam walked back to his own office, his mind traveling back fifteen years ago to when he was a senior in high school. He'd just started dating Portia, the head cheerleader, but was still sneaking around with Leah's friend Summer Jones. Adam had known from the very beginning that Portia would make the perfect wife. But even knowing that he planned to marry Portia once he finished college hadn't stopped him from lusting after Summer.

Sitting down at his desk, Adam opened the top drawer and pulled out a picture Summer had mailed him over a decade ago. It was a photo of a beautiful little girl, then three years old. He'd actually received the photo the day before he married Portia. Adam had hidden in his parents' bathroom upstairs, crying his eyes out as he stared at the photo of the daughter he would never be able to acknowledge as his own. Portia would never accept the truth that he'd fathered a child while they were dating, so he'd kept his mouth shut, just as he had while he watched Portia walk down the aisle toward him the following day.

As the years had passed, it had become easier and easier to keep his mouth shut and let things be the way they were meant to be from the beginning. But when he opened his desk drawer and held the only picture he possessed of a child to whom he owed so much more than he'd ever given, that was when he felt the full weight of his sins.

The phone rang. Adam quickly returned the photo to his desk drawer and answered, "Pastor Adam speaking. How can I help you?"

"I need you to go pick up Winter."

"What?" Had he heard her right? He would curse Leah until the day he died for bringing this woman back into his life.

"You heard me. My cousin is getting evicted. She can't keep Winter for me anymore. And there's no sense in our child being homeless when you have a beautiful home—four bedrooms, from what I hear, and only two kids in the house. Plenty of space for Winter."

"If you hadn't tried to run Solomon down, she would be able to stay with you," Adam reminded her. "What kind of a mother does something like that—especially when her daughter has nowhere else to go?"

"She does have somewhere else to go...with her father," Summer said. "And if you don't go pick her up, I'm going to call that little wife of yours and let her know what's going on."

"You wouldn't."

"Try me."

"Okay, okay. Wait—just wait." Adam held up his hand, even though she couldn't see him, as if to halt the madness swirling around him.

"What am I waiting for, Adam? Are you getting ready to develop a heart or a conscience and start taking care of your kid?"

"Just give me a little time to come up with a solution."

"You've got two days to pick up Winter. If you don't, I'm not just calling your precious wife; I'm calling your dad, too."

She told him she would call him back the next day with the address and then hung up.

⸎

"So nice to have you back, Mr. Harris."

Solomon nodded at his secretary. "It's good to be back, Mary. What's the latest? Anything new?"

"Oh, you know how it goes around here. Everything is an emergency and must be completed ASAP, even if it takes until midnight."

He smiled at Mary. She was thirty-something, with no husband or kids—the type of employee law firms loved. She would work twenty-four hours straight if the team needed her, especially if it would help her get that paralegal position she'd been vying for. "You love every minute of it. Admit it," he teased.

"Yeah, but I'll tell you what I didn't love: hearing about what happened to you on that case out of North Carolina. I've had the whole secretarial pool praying that the police apprehend that woman quickly."

"I've been praying for the same thing," Solomon said. "I doubt she'll come all the way to California, but I think she's unstable enough to bring harm to others, maybe even her own daughter. I would hate for that to happen."

Mary nodded. "And it looks like they're pawning off another losing case on you," she said as she handed him a file folder. It was green, which meant that the client was new to the firm.

"It's that bad?"

"They caught this winner inside his uncle's house, with jewelry in hand when the cops arrived. His uncle had been out of town when the meth head decided to become a jewel thief…at least, that's the story he told the cops."

Solomon raised his eyebrows incredulously. "He confessed?"

"Mm-hmm. Can you believe it?" Mary just shook her head.

"Then why do the bosses want to go to trial on this?"

Mary shrugged. "The kid's family has money and connections."

Solomon carried the folder down the hall toward his office, but he wasn't feeling this case. He knew without even opening the file that the first order of business would be to get the confession thrown out. If the judge miraculously granted his request, then they would claim that the client had had every right to be in his uncle's home. Maybe he was house-sitting, or he stopped by because he saw the lights on and wanted to make sure everything was okay. Blah, blah, blah.

"Was it a cousin?" Mary asked.

"What?" Solomon stopped walking and turned to face his secretary. He'd been lost in thought and hadn't heard the first part of her question.

"The sick family member you visited in Charlotte…I know you don't have any siblings, so I figured it must have been a cousin. How is he or she doing?"

Solomon struggled to come up with a response. When he'd left town, all he'd said to Mary was that he'd needed to visit an ailing family member. He pointed to his office and nearly stuttered as he said, "Let me grab my coffee mug." Then he rushed through the door, set down his briefcase, and gripped the back of his chair, trying to find a way out of this conversation. Then the heavens shined down upon him. He heard a knock, turned, and discovered Lamar leaning against the doorjamb.

"Solomon, my man! How long have you been back?"

Solomon smiled. "About three days. I worked from home so I could let my ribs continue to heal, but I feel as good as new now."

"I was messed up over how that woman tried to run you down after I left town," Lamar said, shaking his head. "After all, I was the one who gave you the information that probably set her off in the first place."

Solomon picked up his coffee mug and moved from behind his desk toward the door. "Don't even think about it. You were just doing your job, as I was doing mine. Neither one of us could have anticipated that woman reacting in such a violent way."

"You headed to the break room for some coffee?" Lamar asked.

"Yeah." Solomon lifted his mug. "Got to get my morning started. I'm playing catch-up. I'm seriously behind on filing my billable hours."

Lamar straightened. "I'll walk with you, because I want to hear all about how the good doctor nursed you back to health."

"You don't know what you're talking about." Solomon breathed easy as he and Lamar walked down the hall. He'd much rather spend his time kidding around with his friend than answering Mary's questions.

"Oh, I know more than you think," Lamar said with a wink. 'I mean, I already figured you were interested in her, but I saw the way she looked at you when you weren't paying attention. She's got it bad, man."

"I think your eyes were playing tricks on you. I've dated women who seemed like they had it bad for me, and Larissa doesn't act anything like them."

"Boy, wake up. You've dated women who had it bad for your title and your potential. That doctor has got her own title already. So maybe she's not fawning all over you and feeding off every word that falls out of your mouth...but, mark my words, she's got something for you." Lamar tapped his knuckles against his heart. "Right here."

In the break room, Solomon filled his mug from the coffee carafe, then turned back to his friend. "You really think so, huh?"

Lamar nodded. "But if you don't know what to do with all the love that fine doctor wants to throw your way, step aside and let a real man take over."

Solomon stood up straight and popped his collar. "Don't get it twisted. I'm all the man that Larissa needs."

"Well, if that's the case, why is she still in North Carolina? She's an entire continent away from the man she 'needs.'"

Deflated, he seemed to shrink as his shoulders slumped. Putting a spoonful of sugar in his coffee, Solomon admitted, "I just don't know if I can deal with the drama that comes with her family."

"A lady that fine has a family crazy enough to make a man want to step back?" Lamar's lip twisted as he shook his head. "Whoa."

"Whoa is right. I just don't know if I need that kind of drama in my life."

As they walked back to Solomon's office, Lamar said, "I had a friend who ended up divorcing his wife because her crazy mama was trying to kill him. The woman would come to their house multiple mornings each week to fix him breakfast."

"That doesn't sound so sinister to me," Solomon said.

"Right. My friend thought he had hit the jackpot as far as mothers-in-law were concerned. Turns out she was lacing the coffee with anti-freeze. He almost died."

"That's a joke, right?"

Lamar raised his right hand in the air. "I kid you not. Right hand to God. To this day, my friend still has trouble digesting food."

"And on that note, I think I'll get back to work and drink my anti-freeze-free coffee." Solomon lifted his mug to his friend as he entered his office.

"Catch you later," Lamar said before heading down the hall.

Around three in the afternoon, Mary rushed into Solomon's office without knocking. "Have you heard?"

"Heard what?"

"That awful woman who ran you down. She just shot someone." Mary's arms were flapping about.

Solomon jumped up. "What? Who? Wait a minute. How do you know what's going on in North Carolina? She *is* still in North Carolina, right?" Solomon's heart rate doubled as dozens of fears raced through his mind. Could it be that Summer Jones had gotten into their building and was, at this very moment, gunning down innocent bystanders on her way to his office?

Mary approached his desk, reached out, and rotated his computer monitor toward her. Then she reached for the keyboard and, as she typed, said, "The girls and I have been keeping up on the Charlotte news ever since your incident, hoping to see the arrest of that awful woman. Here. Read this." She turned his computer screen back toward him again.

Solomon sat back down and began reading the story of Summer Jones's arrest. She claimed that she was just extracting justice because she was tired of not getting any. Solomon looked up at his secretary. "Who did she shoot?" He was almost afraid of the answer.

"The article didn't say," Mary told him. "But I'm sure they will release the name this evening. Probably just trying to notify family or something." She shook her head. "It just doesn't make much sense. But you were right...she was capable of hurting someone else. I just hope that when they lock her up, they throw away the key."

Sitting back in his seat, Solomon felt like the luckiest man in the world. She'd only tried to run him over with a car, not shoot him. That woman had a lot of pent-up aggression. He picked up his cell phone, getting ready to call Larissa, but then his cell started ringing. He checked the screen. It was Larissa.

"Hey—what's going on out there?" Solomon asked when he answered the call.

Larissa was crying.

"Larissa? Are you okay?"

"It's Adam. He—he's been shot. Please come back. Everything is going crazy here. We need you."

As Solomon held on to the phone, listening to Larissa sob like her heart had been broken, he couldn't help but think of Al Pacino in *The Godfather: Part III*. *"Just when I thought I was out...they pull me back in."*

CHAPTER 15

*W*hat Solomon worried about most when he heard that his half brother had been shot was the impact on his father—his heart condition, in particular. How much more could the man take? First, a woman tries to extort money out of him by accusing him of child molestation, and then he discovers that his oldest daughter was behind the whole thing; now, his son had been shot and was just barely hanging on to his life.

And then he wondered how he had gone from barely thinking about David Davison to thinking of him as "Father" and worrying about the things that concerned the Davison family. Solomon closed his eyes as his plane touched down. He was in his father's town again, but it wasn't as if he could get off this plane and proclaim to anyone that he was the son of David Davison. He was getting ready to go to the hospital and sit with the family, meanwhile trying to conceal his identity. That just wasn't cool.

But Solomon put his own feelings aside and hailed a cab. Adam was in trouble, and he was going to help him in whatever way he could. He also needed to get to Larissa and make sure that she was doing better. He, for one, would be doing far better once he was with her.

⌒⌒⌒⌒⌒

Larissa wrung her hands as she paced the floor of the intensive care unit. She didn't know what to do but to call out to the One she had trusted since childhood. So, she left her family and went to the hospital chapel to pray. The place was empty; she sat on one of the pews, alone with Jesus, and gazed up at the wooden cross that was suspended from the wall above the altar.

Tears welled in her eyes and began sliding down her cheeks. Her beloved aunt and uncle didn't deserve the pains and hardships they'd had to endure over the last several months. They were good people who would give the shirt off their backs to anyone in need. Hadn't they taken her in when her parents neglected their responsibilities? Hadn't Uncle David supported Solomon financially? Looking directly at the cross, Larissa screamed out loud, "Why is this happening?"

She got down on her knees, steepled her hands, and then began pouring her heart out to the Lord. "I don't like complaining. I feel as if I was blessed beyond my wildest dreams when I was allowed to stay with my aunt and uncle. They have been better to me than my own parents ever could have been. That's why I don't understand any of this. Adam may not be perfect, but he's a nice guy and certainly didn't deserve to be shot.

"Help us, Lord. If You don't help us, I don't know what we're going to do. If Adam dies, my aunt and uncle will be devastated." The thought of the pain Adam's death would cause her family sent a jolt through her body, and she closed her eyes. She started weeping again as she tried to form the words that were in her heart. She was so overcome with sadness that all she could say was, "I trust You, Lord."

She stayed on the floor, hoping to hear from God. But after about thirty minutes of hearing only the sound of her sobs, Larissa dried her face on her sleeve and stood up. She hadn't heard God's voice audibly, but she was confident that He had heard her prayers, and that knowledge alone was enough.

She headed back to the ICU, praying that Adam's condition had changed for the better since she had been gone. As she rounded the corner and started down the final stretch of hallway, she could see Solomon standing at the nurses' station. "I'm sorry," she overheard a nurse tell him, "but only immediate family is allowed in the ICU."

Solomon looked like he was about to say something but then thought better of it. His expression was that of someone who wasn't sure he belonged. And the impression broke her heart.

Larissa rushed to his defense. "He is family," she informed the nurse as she took hold of Solomon's hand. "Come on, let's go see about Adam."

"Sorry, Dr. Wilkinson," the nurse apologized. "I didn't know." With a sheepish smile, she pressed a button to open the automatic doors to the ICU.

"Thank you for coming," Larissa whispered as she ushered Solomon through the doorway.

"How are you doing?" he asked her.

"Oh, you know. Falling apart. But I think I'll be better now that you're here." She looped her arm through his and leaned her head against his shoulder.

"Have there been any new developments with Adam's condition?"

"He got out of surgery an hour ago," Larissa said. "We're just waiting on him to wake up, and then we'll know…then we'll know." She stopped walking, and once Solomon halted his steps, she put her arms around him and held on like he was her life preserver. "I'm sorry to burden you will all of this. I'm just so scared. If Adam doesn't pull through… I don't know if Uncle David will be able to take a blow like this."

Solomon held Larissa like a fragile doll he was afraid to break. "Don't you ever apologize to me for being scared of losing someone who is like a brother to you. I'm here, Larissa. Lean on me. You don't have to be strong today; I'll be strong for the both of us."

"Thank you, Solomon." She smiled up at him. "Thank you so much for being here."

"Of course." His gaze held such comfort. "Now let's get in there with the rest of the family and find out if Adam has woken up from surgery yet."

Nodding, Larissa released her hold on Solomon. He put his arm around her waist, and they continued down the hall. "You're a good man, Solomon Harris."

He chuckled. "That's not what you said when we first met, but I see that I'm growing on you."

Solomon knew how to make her smile, even in the darkest of times. She loved that about him. She loved him. With that realization, she lost her footing and stumbled slightly.

Solomon caught her with a gentle grip on her arm. "You okay?" he asked.

"Yeah. Just a little clumsy, is all." *And a little bit confused*, she thought as she looked up at him.

Before she had too much time to dwell on the conversation in her head, Tamara ran up to them. "He's awake. He's awake!"

"Oh my goodness!" Larissa cried. "Do you mean it?"

Head bobbing up and down, Tamara said, "Mama and Daddy are in there with him now."

"Where's Portia?" Solomon asked.

"She's at home with their children. She was so shaken up after everything that happened that Mama told her not to drive out here right now."

Solomon and Larissa sat down on one of the couches in the waiting area with Tamara. Leah was hunched in a chair against the wall in a small alcove, her head down, her arms wrapped around herself. She looked like a child who'd been placed in the corner for a time-out.

Solomon tilted his head in Leah's direction. "Why is she sitting over there?" he asked Larissa.

Larissa leaned closer to him. "She blames herself," she whispered. "All of this started because she wanted to get even with her father, and now Adam is fighting for his life."

"That's a lot of weight for one person to hold on her shoulders."

"It is," Larissa agreed. "Why don't you go over there and talk to her?"

"She's not interested in anything I have to say."

"Don't be like that." She nudged him out of his seat. "You might be the one God gives the right words to say."

Solomon didn't know what help he could be to Leah. After all, he was the reason she had taken such drastic measures against her father—*their* father. But Solomon did understand the way she felt, at least partially. She was the child who had always felt left out, just as he had felt for so many years. In fact, he still felt that way.

He crossed the waiting room and sat down next to Leah. When she looked up at him with a question in his eyes, he said, "I thought you might want some company."

Leah scoffed. "Are you sure you want to do that? Being in company with me might get you exiled from this family."

Solomon chuckled. "I've already been exiled for most of my life. Remember me? I'm the half brother you knew nothing about until this year."

"Maybe you're right," Leah said with a sigh. "What else can they do to you besides take you out of the will? The truth is, Adam and I would love it if they did that." Sadness crept into her eyes as she added, "But who knows if Adam will outlive our parents? Maybe it will be his name that's taken out of the will."

"Don't do this to yourself, Leah," Solomon pleaded. "You've got to have faith. I believe that God is able to do the impossible. What about you?"

She shook her head. "I used to believe, but then again, I used to believe in Santa Claus and the Easter bunny, too. Shows how much I know."

"Adam needs you to be strong for him," Solomon told her. "He's in there fighting for his life, and he needs us to be praying and believing that God can bring him out of the nightmare he's in. Do you think you'd be willing to pray with me, Larissa, and Tamara?"

Twisting her lips and twirling her hair around her finger, Leah said, "They don't want me messing up their prayers."

"I don't think you'd be messing anything up. And I think Larissa and Tamara need just as much support as you do right now. I can see how much you're hurting, and I know that you love your brother and wouldn't have wanted anything like this to happen to him."

She unfolded her arms and turned to Solomon. "Why are you being so nice to me? I sure haven't been nice to you."

"We're family, right?"

Leah nodded without hesitation this time.

Solomon grabbed hold of her hand, helped her stand up, and led her over to where Larissa and Tamara were seated. "Do you two mind if we join you?" he asked them.

Tamara moved over and patted the seat next to her. "Take a load off."

"That's just what we need to do," Solomon said. "Would you two join hands with us as we pray for a speedy recovery for Adam? I think Leah would feel a lot better if we did that."

Larissa popped up from her chair. "Absolutely. I'd love to."

Tamara was a little slower to stand, but she soon clasped hands with Leah and Solomon. "We did a group prayer earlier with Mama and Daddy, but I don't see the harm in praying again."

After the prayer, Solomon opened his eyes and noticed that tears were careening down Leah's face. Larissa reached over and wiped her cousin's cheeks with a tissue. "We've done enough crying for today. Adam is going to be alright. Let's just keep praying for him."

Soon David and Alma came to the waiting area and informed everyone that Adam had drifted back to sleep without telling them anything.

Solomon volunteered to go to the cafeteria to get snacks and drinks for the family. As he was headed back to the ICU carrying a tray full of snacks and sodas, a young girl rushed into the hospital and nearly collided with him. In her effort to avoid him, she lost her balance and fell to the floor. Solomon transferred the tray to one hand and used the other to help her up. "Are you alright?" he asked.

Looking frazzled, she wiped off her pants. "I'm sorry, mister. I didn't mean to run into you."

"It's okay. You didn't do much damage." Solomon smiled, then scanned the area. "Where are your parents?"

Shaking her head, the little girl teared up.

"What's wrong? Did something happen to your dad? Your mom?"

She nodded. "She got arrested."

What had he just gotten himself involved in? "Where's your father?"

"He's here in the hospital," she answered. "I came here to find him because my aunt got evicted. She doesn't have a place for me to stay. If I can't go with my dad, I don't know what I'm gonna do."

"Does your dad work here?" Solomon asked.

She shook her head.

"Then why do you think he's here?"

"'Cause the hospital called and said he was. He's in intensive care."

Great, Solomon thought. He could help this little girl on his way back to Adam's room. "That's where I'm headed," he told the girl. "Let me take you there. The nurses should be able to direct you to his room."

"Thank you so much, mister."

"Do you need to wait on whoever brought you here?" Solomon asked, glancing at the door. "Is somebody parking the car?"

The girl shook her head. "I need to get to my dad."

"Okay, then. Follow me." They walked to the elevators, and Solomon pushed a button. "If your father's in intensive care, how will you be able to stay with him? You don't intend to spend the night at the hospital, do you?"

"I don't know, mister. I just need to talk to him and convince him that my mom didn't shoot him so she can come back home."

Solomon stopped in his tracks. He turned to the little girl. "What's your father's name?"

"Adam Davison."

CHAPTER 16

Solomon almost tripped over his feet when the girl told him that her father was Adam Davison. After regaining his wits, he called Larissa and asked her to meet him in the cafeteria. He then turned back to the young girl and asked, "Are you hungry?"

"I'm alright," she said, but the grumbling of her stomach belied her cool demeanor.

The kid was one tough number, but Solomon had seen this act on a number of the children he mentored through the youth program at his church. They started off claiming that they didn't need anything—that they could take care of themselves. But give them a hug and tell them about the love of Christ, and for most of them, the hard exterior would begin to melt away. Kids just needed to believe that somebody cared about them.

"Here, take this." Solomon lifted his ham and turkey sandwich off the tray and handed it to her. "I saw how you were eyeing my food. I know you're hungry. It's okay."

She unwrapped the sandwich quickly and bit into it like it was the first thing she'd had to eat all week. Solomon shook his head. He'd never understand why people who didn't know the first thing about taking care of children were able to have so many of them. That was one of the things he planned to ask God about when he made it to heaven.

"Solomon?" Larissa said as she approached the table. "What's going on?"

He handed the girl his orange soda and directed Larissa to a corner where he could speak privately but still keep an eye on the little girl.

"Why are you sitting down here with Summer's daughter?"

"I didn't ask her name yet, but I figured that I had just met Winter. Am I correct?"

Larissa nodded. "What does she want?"

"You're not going to believe this."

Larissa glanced over her shoulder at Winter, then turned back to Solomon. "Try me."

"She says that Adam is her father."

Larissa's head almost swiveled around. "What?"

"You heard me. She also says that her mother didn't shoot Adam."

"Then who did? The Easter bunny?"

Solomon shrugged a shoulder. "I don't know. But the one thing I do know is that this little girl's mother is in jail, and she has nowhere to live. If we don't help her, she'll be out in the cold tonight."

"Call Child Protective Services," Larissa said, lowering her voice. "They'll take her in."

"What if she is Adam's daughter?" Solomon began.

"She's not."

"But what if she is? Don't you think Adam would want us to look after his daughter rather than send her off to God knows where?"

"Well, what do you suggest, then? Because there's no way that we can take her into the ICU and tell my aunt and uncle that Adam may have an illegitimate child. Not to mention that this is the same child that Uncle David was accused of molesting."

Solomon cleared his throat. "Do you really think they will be shocked by this accusation about Adam? Or will they just think, *Like father, like son?*"

Larissa frowned. "You're not funny in the least bit." Then she got a pensive look in her eyes and tapped her chin. After a few seconds of pondering, she said, "Let me take those sandwiches back to the family and make my excuses for leaving. Then I'll take Winter to my apartment. The two of you can stay there, and I'll stay at the house with Uncle David. Hopefully, we can straighten this situation out once Adam wakes up and can talk to us."

"Sounds good." Solomon nodded. "Let's go tell Winter what we're going to do."

They walked back to the table and took a seat. Solomon turned to Winter. "If I heard you correctly earlier, you don't have anywhere to sleep tonight, correct?"

Winter nodded.

"Well, Ms. Larissa is going to let you sleep at her apartment," Solomon said.

With a sparkle in her eyes, Winter turned to Larissa and said, "Thank you so much." Then she looked back at Solomon and asked, "When can we get my mom out of jail?"

⸻

"Please tell me that you aren't even considering helping that child's mother," Larissa said to Solomon. They had just gotten Winter situated in the spare bedroom and were now in the kitchen talking.

"I never told her I would get her mother out of jail," Solomon said. "Once she told me she was at the hospital to see Adam, I was only concerned with keeping her away from David and Alma."

"You believe her, don't you?" Larissa squinted, focusing in on Solomon's eyes, as if by doing so, she could read his mind.

Solomon hesitated only a moment. "I think the situation's entirely possible."

Rolling her eyes, Larissa turned away from him. "You just want to believe the worst of this family, no matter what it is. Isn't that true?"

"No, it isn't. I think the world of you. And earlier this evening, I had a talk with Leah. I don't think she's all bad, just really misguided. But, as a lawyer, I'm trained to go with my gut on certain things, and I knew that something wasn't right with Adam. When Winter said that he was her father, all the pieces seemed to fit."

"What pieces?"

"For one thing, I kept wondering why Adam pawned Winter off on your dad rather than counseling her them himself. But if he had a fling with Summer and knew that Winter was his child, he wouldn't have wanted them anywhere near him. Summer knew that, and I guarantee you that she used it to her advantage."

"But if any of this is true, why didn't Winter mention this during her counseling sessions?"

"Who knows?" Solomon raised his palms. "Maybe her opportunistic mother told her to keep her mouth shut."

Shaking her head, Larissa folded her arms around her chest. "I still don't believe it. Adam is a family man. Portia and his kids mean everything to him. He wouldn't put his relationship with them in jeopardy over a fling with a woman like Summer."

"Oh, don't kid yourself. Women like Summer and my mother attract plenty of attention from men. And those men are willing to do whatever it takes to lay claim to them, even if it means putting their family in jeopardy."

Larissa felt a twinge of guilt. "Solomon, forgive me. I wasn't referring to your mother. I don't know anything about her, but to have raised you to be the man you are, she has to be a very special woman. I don't believe your mother is anything like Summer Jones."

"My mother never lied to me about my father. I always knew that he was married and had another family, and that was why he couldn't come to see me. But one day I asked my mother how she could have gotten involved with someone who wouldn't come see his own kid, and do you know what she said?"

"What?"

"Just that she was young and dumb."

"I know you're not disrespecting your mother by calling her dumb," Larissa said with her hands on her hips.

"No, of course not. My mother is one of the smartest women I know. But, by her own admission, she wasn't very smart when she was young. She told me that it takes life lessons to teach us what we need to move closer to and what we need to stay away from. She gave her life to God a long time ago, and learned those lessons along the way. But Summer is still learning."

Larissa couldn't believe how much credit he was giving that crazy lady. "Need I remind you that Summer is the same woman who tried to run you over?"

"No, you don't have to remind me," Solomon said. "I think her brain is fried. But is she lying about Adam being Winter's father? And did she shoot him?"

"Yes and yes," Larissa said emphatically.

"What if the answer is no and no?"

Larissa threw her hands up in frustration. "Whose side are you on, Solomon? How can you even consider helping this woman? She tried to kill you and my cousin...your half brother."

"I'm nobody to Adam," Solomon said, sounding dejected.

"But he's not nobody to you, or you wouldn't have rushed back here after he got shot."

"I came here for you," Solomon said. "The way you sounded on the phone, I knew you would need me by your side."

Larissa smiled at that. It felt good to know that Solomon cared about the things that concerned her. What didn't feel good was his interest in Summer Jones's guilt or innocence. "Just leave it alone, okay?" she pleaded. "Don't bring shame to your own family by helping this woman any further."

"How can I bring shame to this family when no one outside of it even knows that I'm a part of it?"

"Uncle David knows. Aunt Alma knows. And I think they both would be disappointed if you represented this woman." Larissa paused, praying Solomon would see things her way. "And would it be a conflict of interest for you to testify against Summer for trying to run you down when you're already the attorney of record for Uncle David's case against her?"

Solomon shrugged. "If I decide to take the case, I'll figure out a way around it."

"And what about me?" Larissa's voice was choked with emotion. "How are you going to figure out a way around the fact that I'll probably never speak to you again if you do this to my family?" She was almost whispering.

Solomon dropped his head. "Now that's a problem I have no answer for."

CHAPTER 17

Solomon was seated in the visitation area at the prison, waiting on Summer Jones to be brought down for their meeting. Even though he was not yet the official attorney of record, this particular facility allowed attorneys to meet with their clients in a private room, which was always a plus. Anything that an attorney learned from his client in preparation for representation was privileged information, and the attorney could not be compelled by a judge to repeat said information. But if he met with the client in an open visitation room, where a jailhouse snitch just happened to be conducting a visit of his own, and the snitch overheard the conversation, the information could be used to extort a plea deal from the prosecutor, and Solomon would be powerless to do anything about it.

The door opened, and Summer was brought into the room in the normal jailhouse jewelry that went so well with the orange jumpsuit. The instant she saw Solomon, she stopped and tried to back up. "I'm not meeting with him."

"What are you talking about?" the guard asked. "He's your attorney, and he looks like a pretty good one, if you ask me." He shoved her back inside the small box of a room and closed the door.

"He's no attorney of mine," Summer objected.

Solomon stood up. "Your daughter asked me to take your case. I agreed to at least come down here and listen to your side of the story. Oh, and by the way, Winter is doing fine. She's staying at Larissa's house, in case you're interested." Solomon didn't like this woman one bit. Any mother who would put her own child's safety in jeopardy because she couldn't control herself long enough to act like a civilized person didn't deserve to have kids in the first place, as far as he was concerned.

"At least somebody in that family is willing to do something for their kin." Summer raised her chin defiantly and glared at Solomon as she took a seat across from him.

"The jury is still out on whether Winter is 'kin' or not," Solomon said, "but we didn't want to see her on the street, where you left her."

"I left her with my sister," Summer said through clenched teeth. "It's not my fault that girl can't figure out how to pay her rent on time."

"Whatever you say." Solomon wasn't going to argue with this woman. He was here as a favor to Winter. Something about that child spoke to him. Maybe it was the fact that she seemed to be alone in the world and needed someone to care about the things that concerned her. Or maybe it was that she was, like Solomon, a child whose father had abandoned her in the interest of keeping the knowledge of his indiscretions concealed from his family and constituents. "I'm here because your daughter believes that you are innocent and asked me to help you out," he explained to Summer.

She eyed him skeptically. "Why would you want to help me?"

"I really don't," Solomon admitted. "After all, you did try to run me over with your car."

"You had no right to interfere with the payday I was promised. Winter deserved that money from those high-and-mighty Davisons. None of them ever did nothing for my baby. It was time for them to pay."

"Extortion is usually not the best method for getting money one believes one is due," Solomon said.

Smirking, she told him, "I couldn't afford some high-priced suit like you, so I had to get in where I fit in...you feel me?"

Solomon narrowed his eyes. "No, I'm not 'feeling' that. But let's switch gears for a minute. I've read the police report, but I want to learn as much about this case from you. And let me warn you now: It's no longer my policy to represent liars. So, if you lie to me, I can't help you. Do we understand each other?"

"Does that mean you're going to take my case? Even after what I did to you?"

"I didn't say that," Solomon said, shaking his head. "At the moment, I'm just exploring my options with this case. And I'm fulfilling a promise I made to your daughter. But if you don't think you can be truthful about the situation, I can get up and leave right now. That way, neither one of us will have wasted any time."

"Don't get your shorts all bunched up," Summer protested. "I promise you that everything I say will be the truth."

Solomon nodded, then looked down at his notes. "According to police records, Adam Davison was discovered in your hotel room. Can you tell me about that?"

"There's nothing to tell." She leaned back in her seat. "I didn't do it."

"But he was discovered in your hotel room. How do you explain that?"

"Of course he was discovered in my hotel room. I'm the one who found him and called the ambulance. I left the room and went down the hall to get a bucket of ice. The ice machine on my floor wasn't working. Nothing at that rat hole of a hotel works. So, I climbed the stairs to the second floor and grabbed some ice out of that machine. By the time I got back to the room, Adam was there, lying on the floor. Looked like he'd been shot in the back, so I got out my cell phone and called nine-one-one."

"But you weren't there when the police and ambulance arrived."

Summer rolled her eyes. "I might have been born at night, but I wasn't born last night. I had a warrant out for my arrest. If I would've hung around that place, the cops would've snagged me for sure."

"But they snagged you anyway. And now you have another charge— attempted murder—added to your list." Solomon raised his eyebrows to underscore the gravity of the situation. "If Adam dies, the charges will just keep growing."

"But I didn't do it! I had no reason to kill Adam. He came to the hotel to help me and Winter."

"What kind of help was Adam offering you?"

Summer glanced to the side. "He wasn't doing it out of the goodness of his heart. I called him several times, threatening to expose him if he didn't fork over the cash I needed so that my sister wouldn't get evicted and so I could get out of town."

"That extortion gig of yours again...I believe it," Solomon said. "Continue."

"Anyway," she said, as if she didn't appreciate being interrupted, "my last call got his attention. He came to the hotel to bring me the money. Why would I shoot him when he was providing me a way to get out of town?"

Solomon didn't know how he felt about his half brother giving money to the very woman who had tried to run him down, all so she could skip town and not face justice for her crime against him. But that was a fight for another day. "Did you and Adam get into an argument over the amount he was supposed to give you?" he asked.

"No. I never even saw the money. He knocked on my door as I was heading out for ice. I told him to make himself comfortable and said that I would be a back in a minute."

"Did you talk to anyone when you went for ice?"

She shook her head. "The ice machine was on the other side of the building, and then I went all the way upstairs. I didn't even hear the shot." She thought for a few seconds, then added, "Or maybe I didn't pay attention to it. Shots were always being fired in the spot I was in."

"Okay." Solomon made a few notes on his pad, then looked up at Summer again. "Did you check his pockets and take the money?"

"No. Like I told you, I never saw it. If I had, the cops wouldn't have caught up with me because I would have been in the wind." She hunched her shoulders. "So, yeah, I thought about taking the money off of him and running, but I was afraid to move him. He looked so frail, like he was bleeding out, you know?"

Solomon jotted another quick note. "How long did you wait before calling the police?"

"I wasn't trying to call the police. I dialed nine-one-one as soon as I saw him lying on the floor like that, but I asked specifically for an ambulance."

As Solomon continued writing, he made the decision to believe her about the money. When Summer was arrested, she had ten dollars in her purse. He also believed her because of what Winter had told him about her aunt being evicted. Because if Summer had received the money she would have been able to pay for her sister's apartment and then have plenty left over for her get away. At least, he thought she would have. "How much money was Adam bringing you?"

"I told him that he owed me the other five thou I would have gotten from Leah if everything had gone as planned. And I wanted an extra five for the way he neglected Winter all her life."

Still writing, Solomon said, "Okay. That means that ten thousand dollars just got up and walked out of Adam's pocket, because he didn't have any money on him when he got to the hospital."

"I don't know." Summer shrugged. "Maybe the paramedics took it, because I sure didn't get one red cent of it."

"Okay," Solomon said, shutting his notebook. "I'll tell you what I'm going to do. I'm going to put my investigator on this, and if everything you've told me checks out, then I'll take the case."

"Well then, I guess I've got myself a lawyer, because I've told you the God's honest truth." Then Summer's smile vanished. She looked as if she was about to be sick. "There's just one thing. I…um…I can't pay you anything."

"This one's on me," Solomon said. "Pro bono."

Summer meant nothing to him. But her kid had gotten to him. He would help Summer at no charge, but only because that would bring even the smallest amount of joy to Winter's face.

Summer raised her eyebrows. "And here I thought you were the devil because you had been Pastor Davison's mouthpiece."

"Since you brought him up, there are a few things you'll need to do if you want me to represent you."

"What do I need to do?"

"First off, because there is a conflict of interest in my representing both you and the victim's father, we will need to dispose of that case before we can move forward with this one."

"And how do we 'dispose of' the other case?" Summer was frowning now.

Solomon opened his briefcase and took out a Waiver of Conflict of Interest form. "If you want me to represent you, you'll need to sign this form indicating that you are aware that my previous client was involved in a case against you. By signing this form, you attest that you are waiving any future claims concerning this conflict of interest. Do you understand that?"

Summer waved the notion away as if swatting at an annoying gnat. "Yeah, yeah. Just give me the form already." She grabbed the pen Solomon offered her, signed the form, and handed both back to him.

"There's just one more thing," Solomon said as he slid the form back inside his briefcase.

She folded her arms across her front. "What? You want a kidney now or something?"

Solomon raised an eyebrow. "Being a smart aleck isn't going to get you far with me."

Summer just stared blankly at him. After a few moments, she must have figured out that he wasn't going to say anything without further prodding, she said, "What? Tell me already. Please."

Solomon sighed. "There's the case that you have pending against the state for trying to run me down. Right now, it's another attempted murder case. But I'm sure I can get it pleaded down to vehicular assault. You'll do some time in prison, but not nearly as much as you'd do on an attempted murder charge."

"Why do I have to plead to anything? Why can't we just go to trial on that one, too?"

"I draw the line at defending anyone on a case in which the person tried to cause bodily harm to me. Now, you can take it or leave it."

She thought about it for a minute, seeming to weigh her options. Finally, she nodded.

"When we plea this down, you'll be required to give an allocution."

"Allo—*what?*"

"You will have to stand up in open court before the judge and tell the court exactly what you did. That includes admitting that you were angry at me because I thwarted your attempt to extort money from Pastor David Davison. You will also admit that the allegations you brought against Pastor Davison were nothing more than a lie. That will put an end to my representation of that client, and then I will be able to handle your case without any conflicts. Got it?"

Summer twisted her lips. "What if I don't want to admit to lying?" she asked.

This was nonnegotiable to Solomon. Summer had wrongly accused an innocent man—his client. And before he would lift a finger to help her, she would have to put it on record that David Davison never touched her child in an inappropriate manner. "Then you'll have to take your chances with a public defender." He waited a beat and then asked her, "What's it going to be?"

"Do I have a choice?"

"You always have a choice." Solomon stood.

"Okay. Get me the deal, and I'll say what I need to in court."

⸻

Larissa returned to her apartment with breakfast from McDonald's for Winter and Solomon. However, she was surprised, and somewhat distressed, to discover that Solomon had left Winter there alone.

"What's the big deal?" Winter wanted to know. "I'm fourteen, and more than able to take care of myself."

"Oh?" Larissa feigned shock. "I didn't know that you had a job. Do you want me to take you apartment hunting?"

"You got jokes, huh?" Winter rolled her eyes. "I wasn't talking about money. I just meant that I can watch out for myself while you and

Solomon do what you've got to do. I know how to cook, clean, do laundry… I know. Big deal, right?"

"I guess your mother leaves you to fend for yourself a lot, then," Larissa said as she set the breakfast sandwiches on the kitchen counter.

Winter grabbed a bacon, egg, and cheese McGriddle. "She has to work," she said simply. "It's not like my dad ever offered to help us out or anything."

Larissa chewed her lower lip, deliberating whether she should say what she was thinking. She decided to go ahead. "You do realize that there's a chance Adam Davison isn't your father, right? Just because your mother says he is doesn't necessarily make it so." She wanted to remind Winter about all the false allegations that Summer had hurled at Uncle David, but she was afraid of saying too much and hurting the child's feelings.

She was stunned when Winter took up the subject without prompting. "I know you think my mom is a big liar because of what she said about Pastor David, but she had her reasons for doing that."

I'll bet she did, Larissa thought. "Why didn't you ever mention anything about Adam being your father during your counseling sessions?" she asked Winter.

The girl swallowed a bite of her sandwich and shrugged. "I didn't know."

Larissa eyed her quizzically. "I thought you said that your mother told you Adam was your father."

"That's right," Winter acknowledged. "But she didn't tell me that until last night at the courthouse. Ever since I was little, I used to ask her where my daddy was, and she just never answered. Would tell me to stop worrying about things that I couldn't change…stuff like that. But after she got arrested, she came out with it…said that if she was going to prison, then I would need to go to my father's people so they could take care of me."

"And do you believe her? I mean, about Adam being your father?"

Shrugging again, Summer said, "I don't know. I guess I do. Why? You don't or something? What is it? Don't I look good enough to belong in your family?"

Larissa's heart broke for the girl. She shook her head. "I wasn't thinking anything like that. You're beautiful, Winter. I just wonder why, all of a sudden, Summer would start claiming that Adam Davison is your father."

"Well, there's one way we can know for sure," Winter said.

"What's that?"

"Make him take a paternity test. If he says he's not my father, then make him prove it. It's the least he can do, don't you think?"

Larissa wanted to believe in Adam with every fiber of her being. But what Winter had just asked for didn't seem unreasonable—not by a long shot. Would Adam be willing to take the test?

CHAPTER 18

------◆------

"Good news," Solomon said as he greeted the Davison family at the hospital that evening. They were standing outside Adam's door, waiting to be permitted to visit him.

"This family could use some good news right about now," David said. "Please, sit down and tell us all about it."

"I got the district attorney to accept a plea deal in Summer's case against me, provided she stands up in open court and admits that she tried to run me over because she was upset that I had discovered that her allegations against you were false because she was trying to extort money from you."

"She is going to put that on the record in open court?" Alma asked. The relief in her voice was pronounced.

"She has to tell the truth, or there won't be a plea deal," Solomon affirmed.

"Thank God," David said, looking heavenward. "At least we'll be done with one ordeal involving that woman."

"What were the terms of the deal?" Alma asked.

"The charge was knocked down to vehicular assault, and she'll get anywhere from four to six months for the crime."

"But that woman tried to kill you—just as she tried to kill Adam!" Alma exclaimed. "Don't tell me she's going to get only six months for what she did to him, too." She seemed undone by the news.

"I was willing to let my case go so that we could get her on record admitting to what she tried to do to Pastor Davison," Solomon explained, hoping that the news of his personal sacrifice would soften her reaction a little.

"Well, thank you for that, but it still doesn't seem right," Alma declared.

She didn't seem too interested in turning the other cheek on this one, and for the first time all day, Solomon actually began to wonder if he had done the right thing by even considering taking Summer's new case.

"Did you receive a call from the prosecutor on the case or something?" Leah asked him.

"No; actually, I called him," Solomon answered evenly. Meanwhile, his mind was going a mile a minute, trying to decide the best time to tell them about what else he had been up to. He only hoped that they wouldn't try to get him disbarred for taking Summer's case before finishing with theirs. But Solomon had covered his bases on that. He wouldn't become the attorney of record for Summer Jones until the plea deal had been finalized. That was scheduled to happen tomorrow morning. He could only hope that by then, Lamar would have discovered enough about the case to allow him to make an educated decision about whether to take it.

Before anyone could fire more questions at Solomon, the doctor came out of the hospital room and informed them that Adam was awake and that they could visit with him four at a time. Solomon and Larissa hung back as David, Alma, Leah, and Tamara went in to see him. When they were alone, Larissa pulled Solomon aside. "I stopped at my apartment this afternoon, and Winter wasn't there. Please tell me you know where she is."

"Of course." Solomon nodded. "She was getting a little stir-crazy, so I dropped her off at the mall to meet a friend. I gave her enough money for a meal and a movie. The plan is for me to pick her up after I leave the hospital."

"Why didn't you tell me, Solomon? I was worried sick when she wasn't at the apartment. I thought you might have brought her to the hospital or something crazy like that."

"Why would that be crazy?" Solomon asked, his question deliberately drawn out. "Why shouldn't she be allowed to see her father?"

Larissa put her hand on his shoulder. "I didn't mean that the way it came out. It's just that Adam is in a very fragile state right now. I think we should proceed cautiously."

"So what do you suggest?"

Before Larissa could answer, the other four filed out of Adam's room. "You two better go on in and see him," Leah told them. "The nurse is about to close off his visitations for a few hours."

Larissa grabbed Solomon's hand. "Just follow my lead," she said as they ducked inside the room.

Adam was fully conscious for the first time in days, propped up in his bed by a few pillows. "Looks like somebody is on the mend," Larissa greeted him in a chipper voice.

Adam smiled. "My doctor said that I'm the best patient he's had all year. I plan to be doing somersaults in a couple of days." His voice was hoarse, and he looked drained, but he seemed ready and willing to talk.

"Hold on there, mister," Larissa said with a laugh. "I may not be your doctor, but I am a doctor, and I say rest is best."

"Come on, Larissa," Adam whined. "I got plenty of rest last night and this morning. I slept the whole night through."

"That's why you're able to talk with us in such a manner now. Rest helps to rejuvenate the body."

"Listen to her," Solomon admonished him. "Rest was the only thing that helped me after my accident. Well, the pain pills did wonders, too."

Adam turned to Solomon. "Heard you came back to see about me," he said.

Solomon nodded as he took a seat next to Larissa in the chairs at the foot of the bed.

"I wish I had known you when we were kids," Adam said. "Maybe I would have reacted to all of this better. Maybe we could have been friends."

"You can still be friends," Larissa reminded him, her voice hopeful as she looked from one brother to the other.

Their words sounded good. But he doubted that the Davisons would want anything to do with him once they discovered that he had agreed to take on Summer's case. Solomon comforted himself with the knowledge that his so-called family hadn't wanted anything to do with him for twenty-plus years. He'd survived this long without a family, and he would continue surviving—thriving, even—without them in his life.

Adam reached his hand out to Solomon. "Friends?" he asked.

Solomon held back. He wasn't ready to make any promises just yet. "Before we become friends and all, I have a few questions that I need ask you."

He glanced at Larissa, who smiled with a question in her eyes.

When Solomon nodded slightly, Larissa turned to Adam. "I have a houseguest," she announced.

"Oh, really?" Adam said. "Who?"

"A little girl. Well, she's not really little. She's fourteen. She came to the hospital last night looking for her father. She had nowhere to go because she said that her mother was in jail and her father was in the hospital."

"We've had a couple of kids wander in off the streets at the church," Adam told her. "If we can't locate the parents, we typically call Child Protective Services."

Larissa shook her head. "I couldn't do that with this child."

"Why not?"

Larissa hesitated, and Solomon could tell that she was weighing her options: Tell the man about his daughter, or let him go on blissfully living his life, acting as if the child didn't exist. But Solomon couldn't take the chance that Larissa might choose the wrong option. He didn't want a lifetime of waiting and hoping for Winter. So, he decided to take it out of Larissa's hands.

"She couldn't turn her away because the child was your daughter," Solomon said. "Winter is the one who came to the hospital last night."

For the briefest moment, Adam closed his eyes as if a pain had shot through him. But this pain had nothing to do with the bullet that had been extracted from his body. As he opened his eyes again, Adam put his game face on and turned to face Solomon. "I don't know what you're talking about. The girl Dad was accused of touching is not my child."

"I don't want to upset you, Adam," Larissa said slowly, as if choosing her words carefully, "but Winter and Angel look a lot alike. How do you explain that?"

Adam hunched his shoulder. "Angel looks more like Portia than me. I guess I can't explain something like that."

"Oh, come on, man," Solomon exclaimed, leaping out of his seat. "You know Winter is your daughter."

Larissa stood and put her hand on Solomon's shoulder. "Calm down, Solomon. Winter told me that Summer never told her about Adam until yesterday. Maybe Adam was never told about her, either."

Adam knew, alright. Solomon saw it written all over his face. But if Larissa wanted to deceive herself, who was he to ruin her optimistic view of the world? He reclaimed his seat and let Larissa have the floor.

She turned to Adam. "Have you ever talked to Summer about the possibility of Winter being your child?"

Solomon wanted to remind Larissa that Adam had been shot in Summer's hotel room. Besides the fact that he'd been there to help Summer escape justice for a crime she'd committed against him, Solomon had a problem with the fact that Adam was an associate pastor and had been sneaking around, putting himself in a position to be extorted.

"Why are you asking me these questions?" Adam asked, panic making his voice rise in pitch. "After all the years we spent in the same house, don't you know me?"

"I thought I did, Adam." She was quiet for a few seconds, then said, "You tell me what to do. Should I call Child Protective Services for Winter so they can find her family? Or has she already found her family herself?"

Adam closed his eyes and leaned back against his pillows. "I think I need to rest now."

⌦⌫⌦

After the visit with Adam, Solomon raced to the mall so that he could be there for Winter. The kid needed someone to be there for her. He saw her exiting the movie theater with her friend, Diamond. When the girls noticed him, he saw a smile spread across Winter's face as if she was beginning to realize that she could count on him. He wanted to run over to her and wrap his arms around her. But at fourteen, Winter probably wasn't interested in hugs.

"The movie just ended, and we haven't had a chance to eat yet," Winter told him.

"Come on, I'll take you for pizza," Solomon told her.

Winter turned to her friend, and both girls smiled and glee-fully jumped for joy. But then Winter stopped jumping and turned to Solomon. "Wait a minute. Does this mean I have to give back the money you gave me for our food?"

He shook his head. "Keep it. This is my treat."

He took the girls to a local pizza place, where they ordered two pizzas—one that was half pepperoni and half cheese, the other half Hawaiian with pineapples and ham and half Mexican with hot peppers. The girls also wanted chips, cookies, and sodas. Solomon knew he was spoiling them, but he couldn't help himself. He knew how much it hurt to have a father who ignored your very existence. If he could have, Solomon would have purchased the whole world and gift wrapped it for Winter.

"This is so good," Diamond said. "My mom never would have let me sample all of these pizzas. Your uncle must be loaded."

When Diamond was engrossed in her meal again, Winter leaned over to Solomon and whispered in his ear, "I told her that you're my uncle. That's okay, right?"

Solomon nodded, wishing he could tell her that she didn't have the relationship quite wrong. But he wasn't sure where he stood with the Davisons, especially after consulting with Summer. So, he wasn't about to tell her they were family or make any promises to stay in her life, no matter how desperately he wanted to.

After dinner, Solomon dropped Diamond off at home and then rented a DVD. Winter popped some popcorn at Larissa's apartment, and they tried to watch the film, but she was too busy grilling him for either of them to pay much attention to the movie.

"How was my mom when you last saw her?"

"She seems to be doing alright."

"Did she ask about me?"

Now that he thought about it, Summer hadn't asked about her daughter at all. He had been the one to bring Winter into the conversation.

That woman was a piece of work. She had used her daughter in her scam, but her daughter still loved and cared about her mother's well-being. And she was desperate for even a small morsel of her mother's affection. He'd been like that when he was a kid, always telling himself that his dad was going to come and see about him one day. Little did he know that his father had been lurking around, snapping pictures, but never giving him a morsel of the affection he had longed for.

"We talked about you," he finally told Winter. "She wants to put this ordeal behind her so that the two of you can make a life together."

"I told you she was innocent," Winter said. "Do you believe me now?"

"Can we just watch the movie?" Solomon didn't want to answer that question. Not tonight, when the jury was still out. Lamar was still investigating Summer's story, and only after Solomon had received and read his report would he be able to form an opinion on the matter.

Winter turned her attention back to the movie until she fell asleep, with the bowl of popcorn still in her lap. Solomon moved the bowl to the side table, then stood and covered Winter with a blanket. Then he stepped back and watched her sleep, wanting so much to give her the happy future she deserved.

Solomon had been so busy building a career that he hadn't thought much about a wife and children. But he was beginning to see what he'd been missing. Maybe it was time for a change of priorities.

CHAPTER 19

*D*avid, Alma, and Leah showed up for Summer's big day at court. First was the allocution of her crime against David and Solomon, followed by the arraignment for her alleged crime against Adam. Summer stood next to a public defender for the allocution, because Solomon would not represent her until the first case against her had been closed.

The judge turned to the prosecutor and asked, "Has the defendant been made aware of the aspects of this plea deal?"

The prosecutor nodded. "Ms. Jones is aware that after her allocution this morning, the state is prepared to knock the charges down to vehicular assault with a recommended incarceration period of four months."

The judge then turned to the public defender and asked, "Is your client ready to give her statement concerning the crimes she is being convicted of?"

"Yes, your honor, she is ready."

The judge leaned back in her seat. "You have the floor, Ms. Jones."

The public defender nudged Summer, and she began speaking. "Yeah, well, I guess I'm guilty of trying to run over Solomon—Mr. Harris."

"And what was your reason for doing such a thing?" the judge asked, appearing bored with the matter.

"I was mad at Solom—Mr. Harris, because he basically accused me of lying about what Pastor Davison did to my child. And the fact of the matter is, I did lie. But the person who asked me to lie about it was going to give me some more money after everything blew up in Pastor Davison's face. I was worried that I wouldn't get my payday because of Mr. Harris."

The gavel came down. Then the judge shook her head. "The court is satisfied with the allocution and sentencing. It will be enforced immediately."

The guard stepped forward, took hold of Summer's arm, and moved her back toward the holding cell. Solomon rushed over to the guard and whispered in his ear. The guard took Summer back behind the defense table. The public defender removed himself and Solomon took his place. "Your honor," Solomon said, "we also have the arraignment to deal with for my client."

The judge looked around the room and then pointed at the public defender as he made his way out of the court room. "I thought he was Ms. Jones's attorney."

"He was only representing Ms. Jones for her allocution. I am the person she tried to run down, so I didn't think it proper for me to represent her for that."

"Aren't you worried that she might try to run you over again if this new case doesn't go the way she wants?"

"No, your honor." He glanced at Summer. "I think my client and I have come to an understanding."

Shaking her head again, the judge said, "It's your funeral. Okay, let's proceed."

Before another word could be spoken, Leah jumped out of her seat. "I don't understand what's going on here. How can you represent this woman, Solomon? She tried to kill Adam. Don't you have any loyalty to this family?"

You're one to talk about family loyalty, Solomon thought. If she hadn't been so vindictive, none of these court cases would have been necessary. But he wouldn't bother trying to enlighten her to that fact.

"Order!" the judge barked, banging the gavel. "What's going on?"

"Solomon has no right to represent that woman," Leah shouted. "He's my dad's attorney."

The judge looked at the guard, then pointed in Leah's direction. As the guard walked toward Leah, the judge asked Solomon to explain the situation.

"I was the attorney of record for Pastor Davison against the lawsuit that Ms. Jones wanted to bring against him. However, that lawsuit has been disposed of with Ms. Jones' allocution, and Ms. Jones has signed a Conflict of Interest waiver because she wants me to handle her defense in this matter."

The guard was escorting Leah out of the courtroom as the judge said, "Alright. Then let's get Ms. Jones arraigned." She turned to Summer. "How do you plead?"

"Not guilty."

"You're guilty, alright!" Alma exploded. "Guilty as sin!"

The gavel went down again. "Maybe we'll need to clear out the entire courtroom today." The judge nodded in Alma's direction, and another guard escorted her out.

This wasn't going so well. Solomon had known that the Davisons would be upset, but he'd had no clue that they would practically come unhinged.

"Your honor, we ask that the defendant be remanded to state custody," the prosecutor said. "She tried to kill a man who was only trying to help her, and this help came even after the defendant tried to extort money from that man's father."

"My client is not a flight risk," Solomon insisted. "And let's not forget that she is innocent of these charges until a jury of her peers says otherwise."

"Your client was hiding out, trying to avoid capture after her other crimes," the prosecutor shot back.

Solomon turned to the judge. "The prosecutor is attempting to paint my client in a bad light. He has no idea whatsoever why she was staying in that hotel, and he should not be permitted to spout off such nonsense in court."

The judge raised her hand. "Enough already. Bail is set at one hundred thousand."

"It might as well be a million," Solomon said flippantly.

"Okay, you got it. Bail is set a one million." The gavel came down, and with that, the arraignment was over.

"Do me a favor," Summer whispered to Solomon. "If the prosecutor offers me life, don't encourage them to execute me, okay?"

"Don't get mad at me. I just meant that you wouldn't be able to post bail for a hundred thousand. Was I wrong?"

"Whatever," Summer muttered. "Just don't mess this up." She stood and let the guard lead her away.

But Solomon was wondering just how bad he had actually messed things up as he watched his father walk out of the courtroom. When David reached the door, he turned back and took one last look at Solomon. In his expression, Solomon realized what it would have felt like if his father had been in his life that day he'd wrecked the car and then acted like he had no clue what had happened to it.

Solomon had just sat down with his chicken and black-bean burrito in a booth at the restaurant when his cell phone rang. "Hey, Lamar," he answered. "Thanks for getting back with me so fast."

"Not a problem. I was able to pull the footage from the cameras at that hotel, and I thought you'd want to know my findings right away... not to mention that Harding has ordered me off this case."

"He did *what?*" Solomon was annoyed to hear that. The firm encouraged the junior members to bring in new clients. However, he knew exactly why this one was being frowned upon. It was pro bono.

"You didn't hear this from me," Lamar said, "but if I were you, I'd give him a call as soon as we're finished talking."

"Gotcha. Now what did you uncover?"

"It appears that Summer was telling the truth, based on the footage that I was able to get from the hotel's surveillance cameras. I saw her leave the room with an ice bucket, and then I saw a man come up the stairs and go into her room. Within the span of a minute, he ran out of the room while stuffing something in his jacket that looked very much like a wad of cash."

"So, somebody did steal the money?" Solomon blurted out, then looked around to see who was in earshot of his conversation. He didn't recognize anyone, so he took a bite of his burrito and chewed while he listened.

"There's more," Lamar said. "I had my guy hack into Adam's bank accounts so we could see where the money came from. Five days ago, ten thousand dollars was taken out of his older child's 529 Plan."

Even though Solomon didn't have children, he knew all about 529 Plans. His mother had opened a college savings account for him at their local bank when he was eight. Every month, after she paid the bills, she would deposit whatever was left of his father's child support check into that account. Ten years later, that money had come in handy. His father had forked over any money that his scholarships hadn't covered for room and board, and Solomon had been able to concentrate on his studies without having to worry about getting a job to pay for the small apartment he'd rented while in law school.

"But here's the thing," Lamar continued. "Find the ten thousand dollars, and you'll find your mystery man."

"I'm just wondering how this man knew that Adam was carrying so much money," Solomon mused. "Maybe he followed him from the bank or something."

"That could be, but if I was making such a large withdrawal, I doubt I'd do it out in the open for just anyone to overhear. And I sure wouldn't be counting it in front of the rest of the customers."

"Adam obviously didn't take every precaution, because someone knew he had that money, and he came for it. Makes me wonder if Summer would have gotten popped, too, if she hadn't been out getting ice."

"The guy probably would have shot them both," Lamar agreed. "You know what I'm thinking?"

"Of course I don't. I'm not as smart as you are."

"Yeah, that's why you have your law degree and I do all the sniffing through public trash cans." Lamar laughed at his own joke before continuing. "Maybe someone else hacked into that account. Check with the bank to see if they experienced any problems. If you've got some local hackers on your hands, they might have decided to follow Adam and take the money for themselves."

"Wow." Solomon let the prospect sink in. "I sure hope there aren't any hackers out there that will look into your bank account and then decide to follow you around and pick your pockets. Remind me to take my money out of the bank and just keep it under my pillow from now on."

Lamar chuckled. "It might be safer there. No bank system is hack proof if a hacker is determined enough."

"Thanks for scaring me with the reminder of the criminal society we live in."

"Anything to help, brother. Check your e-mail in a few minutes. I'll be sending the footage over to you." Lamar cleared his throat. "I've got to get off the phone, but remember what I said. You and I haven't talked."

"Understood," Solomon said. "Thanks for helping me out on this one, Lamar. I just hope I didn't cause you too much grief with the bosses."

"Nothing I can't handle, as long as they don't know I kept working on the case after I was ordered off it."

"I got your back. I'll see you when I get back to town." With that, Solomon ended the call. As he sat there finishing his burrito, he became more and more inflamed about the fact that Harding had a problem with him working on a case like this. His client might be poor and unable to pay for legal services, but she was innocent.

Any other time, Solomon would have just waited for Bob Harding to call and inform him of his issues with the case. But not this time. He didn't want to wait another minute to get this out of his system. He picked up his phone again and speed-dialed the office. Once the secretary put him through to Harding, he said, "I just wanted to check in and let you know that I'm making progress with my current case."

"A case we're not getting a dime on," Harding grumbled.

"Just think of all the goodwill the firm will receive once my client is found innocent."

"Ha!" Harding spat. "You actually think that something good is going to come out of this, when you are clearly in violation of your ethical commitment to our other client? Or hadn't you concerned yourself with the signed contract we have with David Davison?"

"I informed my client of the conflict of interest and had her sign a waiver. And I doubt that Pastor Davison is unhappy, because I refused to take on this client until she gave an allocution to having attempted to extort him. His case is all wrapped up with a nice little bow on it."

"Not everything is handled and 'all wrapped up,' Solomon," Harding groused. "I am still not convinced that this case is the right one for our firm."

"She's innocent, sir. Shouldn't that count for something?" Solomon persisted. "I mean, we are defense attorneys. Shouldn't we be ecstatic when we get an opportunity to represent an innocent client?"

"I'm ecstatic when I can pay my bills and take my family on nice vacations. If that doesn't get you excited, as well, then maybe you need to think about going out on your own. That way, you can represent all of the innocent, non-paying customers your bleeding heart desires. Got me?"

"I got you."

"The clock is ticking on this one. Take five more vacations days to wrap this up and then get back to the office and generate some revenue."

Harding cut him off before Solomon could tell him just what he thought about generating revenue off guilty-as-sin clients just because they had trust funds or large bank accounts. But Harding was right about one thing: Solomon had taken the job because he had liked the idea of earning enough money to do whatever he desired. But that had been five years ago. His priorities were changing, along with his mindset on what type of law he wanted to practice. Maybe he should take Harding's suggestion and go out on his own.

It would be risky. He might have to resort to being an ambulance chaser to make ends meet, but for those rare occasions when he ran into an innocent man or woman, he'd be able to take the case and defend his client with everything that God had placed in him, without worrying about whether it would generate any revenue. He almost called Larissa to ask her advice on this whole "going out on his own" thing, but his battery was low, and he hadn't brought his cell phone charger with him. The conversation would have to wait.

He finished his burrito, then left the restaurant to pick up Winter from Diamond's house. It was summer, so she wasn't in school, but Solomon realized that he'd never asked where she went to school or how her grades were; if there were any bullies in her school; if she had a crush on a boy. He wanted to know as much about Winter as possible. It didn't matter if the Davisons ever acknowledged him as family or if Adam ever admitted to being Winter's father. As far as Solomon was concerned, he and Winter were family, and he would fight for her as long as there was breath in his body.

"Did you have fun with Diamond today?" Solomon asked Winter as she got in the car and closed the door.

"Yep. I like hanging out with Diamond because she gets me."

"In what way?" Solomon was curious. Were she and Diamond two birds of a feather because they both got straight A's in school or because they liked to skip class and hang out with boys?

"Her dad is married, too. She told me that her mom has been trying to break up her daddy's marriage for fifteen years, but he still hasn't budged."

"You'd think she'd give up."

"You'd think she wouldn't have messed with him in the first place," Winter countered. "I swear, I don't understand women like Diamond's mom. At least my dad wasn't married when my mom hooked up with him."

Solomon's mother had made the same mistake as Diamond's. David had been separated at the time, but she'd been well aware that he was married. She'd just been foolish enough back then to believe that "separated" was as good as "divorced." But there was a world of difference between the two.

"Sometimes people make mistakes," Solomon told her. "My mother dated a married man just like Diamond's mother did. Consequently, I grew up without a father."

Winter swiveled her entire body and stared at him for a moment, her mouth hanging open. "You're just like me," she finally said. "No wonder we get along so well."

Solomon only nodded, but he was thinking, *More than you know, Winter. More than you know.*

Chapter 20

The breath was almost knocked out of his body when he and Winter returned to Larissa's apartment, opened the door, and came face-to-face with some angry Davison women. Alma, Leah, and Tamara were seated around Larissa's octagonal dining room table. Not wanting to subject Winter to anything they might have to say, he turned to the girl and said, "Why don't you go to your room? You can watch TV or play that video game you suckered me into buying."

"Where's Larissa?" Winter asked as she looked around the room.

"She's at work," Alma said, "but I've sent word and asked her to meet us here. Now you run along and do as Solomon told you."

"But don't you want to talk to me?" Winter asked Alma.

Solomon put his hands on Winter's shoulders and turned her toward the bedroom door. "Not now, Winter. We'll discuss this later."

"Alright, alright. I'll go." Winter huffed off to her room.

After Winter had closed the bedroom door, Solomon turned his attention back to the women. The table would sit four, but he didn't feel comfortable taking the vacant seat, so he leaned back against the counter and faced his accusers. "How did you all get in here?"

"A more appropriate question would be, why are you and that...that *girl* in my cousin's apartment?" Leah asked.

"That 'girl' has a name. You certainly didn't mind using it when you hired her mother and used Winter in the process," Solomon reminded her.

"I never meant for any of this to happen," Leah insisted. She turned to her mother. "Mama, you've got to believe me. I will never do anything to harm this family again. I'm not the traitor." She looked back at Solomon and pointed an accusatory finger. "*He is.*"

"Yeah," Tamara piped up. "Solomon, I know you're angry about not having Dad around when you were a child, but how could you do something like this to your brother?"

"What exactly do you think I'm doing to hurt Adam?" Solomon asked her.

Alma's facial expression said *"Duh!"* "You're defending the woman who tried to kill him. She also tried to kill you and defame David's good name, I might add."

Solomon shook his head. "She's guilty as sin on your last two points, but she didn't shoot Adam."

"Then why did Adam say she did?" Leah demanded.

"That's something you'll have to ask him. But, trust me, I have all the proof I need that my client is innocent."

"Why would Adam lie?" Tamara asked.

"Again, that's something you'll have to ask him," Solomon said.

Tapping her fingers on the table while eyeing Solomon, Alma said, "Okay, I'll ask Adam. But you tell me this." She pointed in the direction of Winter's bedroom. "Why has Larissa given this child, who accused my husband of unspeakable acts, a bedroom in her home?"

"Winter never accused your husband of anything. Winter's mother and Leah cooked that scheme up." Solomon nodded toward Leah, so that no one would forget where the scam had originated.

"Point taken," Alma said evenly. "But I know Larissa. She wouldn't just open her home to someone connected with a scheme to hurt her uncle. You must have put her up to this, and I want to know why."

Larissa picked that moment to open the door. She stood in the entryway and stared at the gathering in her dining room. "What's going on here?"

"You ambushed me, that's what's going on," Solomon said, giving her a look that showed his disappointment.

Flinging her purse on the sofa, she said, "I didn't ambush you." She pointed at the women seated around the table. "*They* ambushed *us*. My aunt has a key to my apartment. She called and told me to meet her here. I've been calling your cell phone for the last forty minutes, but it's been going straight to your voice mail."

She had him there. He had forgotten to charge his phone the night before, and the telephone calls with Lamar and Bob Harding had drained the last of his battery. Thinking of them reminded him of the file Lamar said he would be sending. Solomon opened his briefcase and pulled out his iPad.

While he was checking his e-mail, Leah pounced on Larissa. "Why is Summer's daughter staying in your apartment? How ungrateful can you be? My parents take you in, and you harbor the daughter of the woman who tried to kill my brother?" Leah was close to hysterics.

Winter burst from the bedroom. "Don't you yell at Larissa!" she shouted. "She is kind and sweet…not like you."

Leah shrunk back a second, then seemed to regain her bearings as she struck back, "You are a hateful little girl who doesn't know how to stay out of grown folks' business."

"Don't you talk to her like that." Larissa stood in front of Winter, protecting her like a mother hen. "You want to lash out at me, then go ahead. I'm not afraid of you and your venom. But don't you dare inflict your ugly attitude on this innocent child."

"Innocent my foot," Leah spat. "She's up to her eyeballs in this, right with her mother."

"Leah, please sit down," Alma said, then turned to Larissa. "I knew something was going on when you started spending the night at our house and Solomon was nowhere to be found. I figured that he must be staying at your apartment, but I never imagined that this child was here with him."

Leah may have been more high-strung and out of control with her issues of unforgiveness than her mother, but the base issue was the same, as far as Solomon was concerned. Alma was the reason he'd never had a relationship with his father. She couldn't forgive then, and it didn't appear that she wanted to forgive now. Harboring bitterness against an innocent child who had no control over her mother's actions.

Solomon wasn't going to let this happen. He was putting a stop to it, right here and now. "Before you say another word, Alma, you might be interested to know that Winter is Adam's daughter, and Larissa has allowed her cousin's child—your granddaughter—to stay in her home because she has nowhere else to go. So, would you rather see your granddaughter homeless, begging on the street? Or was it a good thing that Larissa opened her heart and her home to Winter?"

The silence in the room was almost painful as Alma stood up and slowly walked over to where Winter and Larissa stood. She took hold of the child's arm, pulled her from behind Larissa, and just stared at her for the longest time. Soon tears started rolling down Alma's face. She closed her eyes and backed away from the child.

"What is it? What's wrong, Mama?" Tamara asked as she held on to Alma and guided her to the sofa.

With her head in her hand, Alma told the group, "When I first saw her, about a year ago at the church, I remember stopping in the hallway and watching her walk by. Something was so familiar about her. Now I know what it is."

"Are you saying that what Solomon said is true?" Leah asked.

When Alma nodded in affirmation, Leah looked even more confused. "How can this be?"

Alma sighed. "I don't know. But I intend to ask your brother about it today." She turned and looked at Winter again. "I need to talk to Adam."

"While you're talking to him, you might want to ask why he lied to the police," Solomon said. He was watching the footage Lamar had sent to him.

"What are you talking about?" Leah demanded. "What reason would Adam have for lying to the police?"

"He told them that my mom shot him," Winter piped up, "and that wasn't true. She's the one who called for the ambulance for him."

Alma turned to Solomon with a questioning glance.

"You don't have to take Winter's word for it. Or mine." He placed his iPad on the dining room table and clicked *Play*. "See for yourself."

Everyone's eyes were fixed on the screen as an image of Adam knocking on Summer's hotel room door came into focus. The door opened, and Summer walked out of her room carrying an ice bucket. Adam went in.

"Stop it! Just stop it!" Alma squealed, covering her eyes with her hands. "I don't want to see another second. What in the world was Adam doing meeting up with that woman at some hotel?"

Solomon paused the video. "He wasn't meeting up with her for what you think." He glanced at Winter and said, "You may want to go back to your room for the rest of this conversation."

Rolling her eyes, she said, "I'm fourteen, Solomon. I can handle whatever you have to say. Besides, I'm not blind. I know that my mother is no angel."

Solomon nodded, then proceeded to explain. "Just as Summer tried to extort money from Pastor David, she was playing the same card with Adam. Only this time, she was threatening to tell the world that they had a daughter. So, Adam brought her the ten thousand dollars she had requested for keeping quiet."

"If he brought her the money, then why did she shoot him?" Tamara wanted to know.

"I think what Solomon has to show us will in some way prove that she didn't," Larissa said. She looked at her aunt. "Don't you want to know the truth, Aunt Alma?"

Alma glanced at Larissa, then reached forward and hit the button to resume running the footage. Everyone watched in silence as a man walked into Summer's hotel room. Nothing else happened for the longest time, and then the man ran out of the room, stuffing something into his jacket pocket.

"I know him," Leah said as she jumped out of her seat.

Tamara turned an accusing eye toward her sister.

"Not 'know him' as in 'hired him as a hit man,'" Leah clarified. "I've seen him before; I just can't remember where or when."

The group watched as Summer came back to the room, then ran out again, screaming for help. Then she rushed back into the room and out again after a few moments.

As the video stopped, Solomon told them, "Summer called the ambulance when she went back into the room. If she had just run off and left him there, Adam would be dead."

"Why did she run?" Larissa wanted to know.

"She had a warrant out for her arrest. Adam was bringing her money so that she could get out of town before the police caught up with her. The hotel clerk saw Summer run away and told the police about it when they arrived. He evidently hadn't noticed the man who came running down those stairs before her."

"How come the police don't know about this man who went into Summer's room and apparently shot Adam?" Tamara asked.

"I don't think they pulled the footage," Solomon said. "Once the hotel clerk told them that he saw Summer running from the scene of the crime, it was probably a wrap from there."

Winter started jumping around the room. "I knew it! I knew it!" she shouted jubilantly. "Didn't I tell you? My mom is innocent."

"So what do we do now?" Alma asked.

"I will be turning over my evidence to the district attorney's office," Solomon told her. "But first I'd like to find out why Adam lied about Summer. If we can get him to recant his story, I might be able to get Summer home to her daughter after she serves those four months for trying to run me down."

All of a sudden, Leah snapped her fingers. "Now I remember where I saw that guy. At Adam's wedding." Then her expression changed from alert to alarm. "Oh my goodness."

CHAPTER 21

*E*verything is falling down around us," Alma said to David after venting to him about all that she had seen and heard that morning.

"And it's my sinful deception that's to blame," David told her. "The chickens have finally come home to roost. We tried to raise our children up to be moral, caring human beings, but I was hiding my sins, and it was only a matter of time before they'd catch up with me."

Alma shook her head. "You are a good man, David. I won't let you put all of this on your shoulders. It's too burdensome."

"How can I not, Alma? I have a granddaughter with whom I've never had the opportunity to build a relationship. Can I blame Adam for that when I did the same thing with my own son?"

"We were young, David."

"No, no. I'm done making excuses. We need to repent, and that's all there is to it." He stood up and entered their walk-in closet, selected a pair of black slacks and a polo shirt, and walked back out again.

"Where are you going?" Alma asked.

"To have a talk with both of my sons. We are going to clear up all of this stuff once and for all."

She put her hands on his shoulders. "David, I don't want you going out there and getting all worked up."

"It's long past time for that. This family has lost its way. And it's time for us to get back what we've lost." He gave his wife a determined look so she would know that his decision was final. "Do you understand what I'm telling you, Alma?"

She sat down on the bed and stared up at him, wide-eyed. She looked almost frightened.

"Even if it means losing the ministry, I'm determined that this family will get right with God," David said. "I hope you're going to be with me on this, because these next few days are going to be some of the hardest days we have ever dealt with."

Alma gulped. "What are you planning to do?"

David held out his hand to her. When she took it, he drew her to her feet again. "You and I have been together for over thirty years. Have I done enough in those years to earn your trust?"

Without hesitation, Alma nodded.

"Then I need you with me. Just follow my lead. Because no matter how any of this turns out, as long as I've got the prettiest woman in the South on my arm, I can weather it all."

Alma gave a slight smile. "I'm with you, David. You never have to worry about me. Go on and do what you have to do. If things don't go well out there, don't you worry about a thing, because I'll still be here when you get home. From this day forward, David, I plan to be a true partner in this marriage. Accepting the good and the bad."

"How on earth did a country boy like me get so lucky to meet a woman like you?" He bent down and kissed his wife like he hadn't kissed her in years.

"Luck had nothing to do with it," Alma told him. "You have always been my gift from God."

David liked the sound of that. He only prayed that Alma would still consider him a gift from God when all was said and done.

⌒⌒⌒⌒⌒

"Are you telling me that if you had a child of your own, you'd let her pick any skimpy outfit she wanted and just go ahead and pay for it?" Solomon was incredulous.

Larissa chuckled. "You're being silly, Solomon. The dress Winter wants is not skimpy. It might be a little form fitting, but she's a teenager. You can't expect her to dress like she's a kid from the fifties."

Larissa and Solomon had taken Winter and her friend Diamond to the mall to pick out a few outfits that were badly needed. Winter's shoes were worn down on the right side, and her jeans were torn from too many washings rather than any fad that the kids had going on these days.

Solomon glanced around the store. "And where did miss hot-pants run off to, anyway?"

With a knowing grin, Larissa said, "I think she and Diamond saw a cute boy from their school." She pointed in the direction of the food court.

"I'm going to get her."

Larissa grabbed hold of his arm. "You'll do no such thing. Let's just pay for the items she's already tried on, and"—she pulled a baby-blue sweater off the rack—"let's add this to the stack. It's perfect for her."

Solomon twisted his lips as he studied the sweater. "Can't they make these things long enough to cover the midriff?"

Shaking her head, Larissa walked to the register. "This sweater will cover her midriff, and you know it."

"You're just too liberal, that's your problem," Solomon said as he pulled out his billfold.

"And you've put on blinders where Winter is concerned and forgotten your teenage years."

After they'd paid for the items, they carried the bags out of the store and strolled along at a leisurely pace toward the food court. Solomon put his arm around Larissa. "I'll tell you what," he said, pulling her closer to him, "if there had been a girl who looked like you in my high school, I probably would have flunked all my classes, no matter what she wore."

She laughed. "You don't have me fooled, mister. You were a ladies' man, and you know it."

Solomon stopped walking, cupped Larissa's cheek with his palm, and looked into her eyes. "I'm serious, Larissa. I've never met anyone who makes me feel the way you do."

That afternoon, Solomon received a call from David asking him to meet him at the hospital. Adam was now out of intensive care and had his own room. When they met in the hospital parking lot, David broached the subject Solomon had been dreading. "I now understand why you would take on Winter's case," he said. "I was confused and disappointed at first, but I wanted you to know that I think you're doing the right thing."

Solomon couldn't believe his ears. "Thanks for saying that." He didn't know why, but having this man's approval meant a lot to him.

When they reached Adam's room, he was alone. Apparently his wife had come to see him in the ICU only once. Solomon had initially found that strange, given how close Adam and Portia seemed to be. But now, after Leah's revelation the day before, he understood.

"Hey, Solomon, Dad," Adam said when they entered the room.

"Hey yourself, Son," David greeted him. "How are you feeling today?"

"Like I've been shot but am on the mend." He shrugged. "At least it doesn't hurt as bad as it did a few days ago."

"That's good to hear," David said as he and Solomon took a seat.

The three men talked a little while longer about Adam's health, and then David switched subjects. "Son, can you help us understand why you told the police that Summer Jones shot you?"

"Because she did," Adam said, instantly defensive.

Solomon held up a hand, stopping Adam before he could go any further. "We obtained a videotape from the hotel's surveillance system. It was a man who shot you, and he looked nothing like Summer."

"She hired him. She must have. Why else would that man come into her room and shoot me like that?" Adam demanded.

"Leah recognized the man, Adam," David told his son. "Are you sure you want to stick with this story? If you don't speak up, a woman is about to go to prison, and a child will be without her mother."

Adam turned to face the wall. "What do you want from me, Dad?"

"I want you to be honest—not just with us but also with yourself. This family can't go on hurting people the way we have. Not any longer."

Adam faced his father again, blinking back tears. Whether they were genuine, Solomon couldn't tell. "But Dad, you've built so much. I can't just mess all of that up for you."

"The Davisons will be okay, Son." David put his hand on Adam's shoulder. "As long as we have God on our side, nothing else matters. I will walk through the fire with you, but you've got to come clean."

"All my life, I've only wanted to make you proud," Adam said. Now the tears were cascading down his face. Probably difficult to fabricate.

"You have, Son. You have."

Almost involuntarily, Solomon's body jerked every time David called Adam "Son," as much as he tried to control it. David must have noticed, because he turned to Solomon and asked, "Are you okay?"

Solomon forced a smile and nodded.

Turning back to Adam, David said, "We've got all night, Son. If you want to wait awhile, we'll be here."

With the sleeve of his hospital gown, Adam wiped the tears from his face. Then he glanced over at Solomon. "Never in a million years would I have guessed that you had a secret child."

David sighed. "I know I wasn't honest with you, Son, and I hope that you will forgive me. Only God is perfect. That's why we have to be careful who will idealize. Sinful man will always let us down in some manner."

"I've let a lot of people down, that's for sure," Adam admitted.

"Adam, before you tell us anything, I want to make sure that you are aware that I am representing Summer," Solomon told him. "So, if you want me to step out of the room so you and Pastor David can talk, I can do that."

Adam chuckled softly, then burst forth in a full-out belly laugh. He held his stomach, as if trying to compose himself. It took a few seconds, but he was finally able to get himself under control.

Solomon and David exchanged glances of confusion.

"Just what is so funny?" David asked Adam with furrowed brow.

"It cracks me up every time Solomon calls you 'Pastor David.' Here I am, thinking how much of an honor it is to have a man like you as my father. Meanwhile, it seems that Solomon couldn't care less. He doesn't need to throw your name around to get into certain circles or to cinch an accomplishment." Adam took a deep breath and leaned back against his pillows. "How freeing that must be."

"You can be just as free as Solomon," David told him. "Think about it, Son. If you didn't care about the weight my name carries—if you didn't feel as if you had to uphold the Davison reputation—what would you tell us right now?"

Adam wiped away his tears once more and looked his father in the eye. "I'd tell you that I feel like a sinner most of the time. I don't know if I picked the right woman to marry." He was blubbering as he added, "And I don't know if I was truly called to the ministry."

David stood up and put his arms around his son. "Step into the fire, Son. I'm here with you."

"I—I've been so afraid of being found out for so long. Summer has blackmailed me off and on for many years. But then she left me alone, and I thought I was in the clear until she showed up at the church."

"What happened, Adam?" David asked, his arm still around his son.

"I swear I didn't know what Leah and Summer had planned. But Summer came to my office one day and told me that I just *had* to get her and Winter in to see you. Said I owed her that much since I barely made my child-support payments."

"Are you saying that Winter is your child?" David asked calmly.

Adam nodded soberly. "I believe she is. Summer wasn't the person she is today when I first got to know her. She was innocent and sweet. But I left her to raise our child on her own because I thought you and Mama would approve of Portia, since her parents were ministers."

"You might want to take a paternity test, just to settle the whole matter in Winter's mind. I think you owe her that much," Solomon suggested.

Adam nodded. "I'll take care of it."

"You really missed out on getting to know a great girl," Solomon told his half brother while shaking his head. "Even with all she's been through, Winter is a first-class kid."

"I'm sure she is. But Portia never would have accepted her. I tried to send what money I could to Winter, but Portia spends like we have an endless supply. She also keeps a close eye on our bank accounts, so it became impossible to withdraw money without her knowing. I guess that's how she knew I took ten thousand out of the kids' college fund." Adam shook his head. "Portia had her cousin follow me. When he came into the hotel room and found me there, he assumed I was having an affair with Summer, so after he'd taken the money from me, he shot me."

"All this time, you knew your shooter, yet you deliberately lied to the police?" Solomon asked, trying to keep the anger out of his voice.

"I didn't want Portia to get into trouble," Adam said. "Despite our differences, she is the mother of my children."

"Isn't Summer also the mother of one of your children?" David asked him.

"She is, but I guess it just feels different since I never had a relationship with Winter."

"It's not different, Son. I never had a relationship with Solomon, but that doesn't change the fact that I would give my life for him in a heartbeat, if need be, just as I would do for any of my other children."

It felt strange for Solomon to hear David say that he would give his life for him, and he wasn't entirely sure he believed it. But maybe he meant it. After all, David Davison was no ordinary man. He hadn't fathered a child out of wedlock and simply forgotten about his existence, all the while praying that his deeds didn't catch up with him. No, he had kept tabs on Solomon. But from a distance. That was the part that bothered Solomon the most. Sometimes he felt that it might have sat better with him if his father had ignored him entirely rather than approached close enough to watch his football games but never stepped forward and made a connection.

They were silent as they headed down to the parking garage after their visit with Adam. Once they reached the cars, David said, "I want to have my granddaughter with me. Do you mind bringing her to the house tonight?"

Solomon smiled. At least he was ready to acknowledge one of his illegitimate offspring. "I think Winter would like that."

"And what about you, Solomon? Would you like to come stay with your old man? Your case should be wrapped up soon, but I was hoping that you'd stay at the house with us for a few days before you headed back to California."

Solomon pressed his lips together, thinking a moment. Was he ready to move into the family mansion, even if only temporarily? Was he prepared to experience the home environment he might have had if he had been raised alongside his half siblings? He probably wouldn't know until he tried. Finally, he made his decision. He would do it, but only because he didn't want to be separated from Winter. The two of them had grown close, and she probably wouldn't feel comfortable without his presence, anyway.

"Fine," he said to David. "I'll go get our things from Larissa's and meet you at the house."

CHAPTER 22

As David had predicted, once Solomon went to the district attorney with his evidence and Adam's sworn statement recanting his earlier claim, the charge against Summer of attempted murder was dropped. Within two days, Portia's cousin Ray-Ray was picked up by the police. According to the report, he hadn't named any accomplices. But Solomon knew that Portia had probably stashed her children's ten-thousand-dollar college fund someplace where she alone could access it.

Adam had obviously made a giant miscalculation when picking as a wife the woman he'd thought was most like his mother. He looked at the outward appearance and hadn't paid much attention to what Portia's insides were made of. She wasn't the type of woman who could forgive and forget, and Adam would have to live with that knowledge for the rest of his life. Whether he and Portia would be able to live together forever was a whole other matter.

Solomon glanced over at Larissa, wondering if he really knew what kind of woman she was inside. Could he count on her, come what may, or would she turn on him if things weren't always coming up roses? That was something he needed to know, because Solomon had pretty much made up his mind to leave People, Smith, and Harding to start his own law firm. And even though he had a fat savings account, things always happened when you owned your own business, and the money could dry up fast. How would Larissa feel if she found herself married to a man who couldn't even carry the mortgage without help?

"Penny for your thoughts," Larissa whispered.

They were at the movies, watching an action flick that didn't have enough action to keep Solomon's mind from wandering and daydreaming about things that might never happen. He smiled at her. "It'll cost you more than a penny. Too much on my mind."

"Shhh," someone behind them said.

Larissa and Solomon giggled like high-school sweethearts as they turned their attention back to the movie. But afterward, when they were at a restaurant stuffing their faces with deep-dish pizza, Larissa came back to her question. "I didn't mean to cause a disturbance inside the movie theatre, but I really was curious. You had such a serious look on your face, like you had just been charged with saving the world from a missile launch that was headed straight for us. Do you want to talk about it?"

Putting his fork down, Solomon decided it was time to tell Larissa all that was in his heart. "I kind of wish we were at a nice five-star restaurant instead of a pizzeria."

Larissa smiled as she looked around. "I like this place. Their pizza is the best in town."

Solomon reached across the table and took her hand in his. Making sure to look her in the eye, he confessed, "I met you at a time of uncertainty in my life. I've been trying to figure out if I want or need a relationship with a someone who basically abandoned me when I was a child. And for the last year or so, I've been feeling as if God has been trying to move my career in a different direction. With all the uncertainty in my life, my blood pressure should be sky high, but you have made these issues easier to deal with. To be honest, it feels like I have a little piece of heaven when I'm with you."

"Oh, Solomon." Larissa gave him a shy smile. "You are a wonderful man, and I feel—"

Solomon lifted his free hand. "Wait. Please let me finish. I need to tell you this before I lose my nerve or convince myself that what I'm feeling isn't real." He took a deep breath and then quickly said, "I'm feeling you, Larissa. You're everything I've ever wanted. But I'm scared to death that I might be just like my father, which means I will end up hurting you. And I couldn't deal with that."

"Wow. You were thinking all that while we were watching that boring movie?" She giggled. "I wish you would have told me right away. We could have walked out of the movie and gone somewhere to talk about this."

The sound of her words was as sweet as honey dripping from a hive, and he leaned in closer, wanting to soak it all in. "Tell me now."

"How could you not know how I feel about you, Solomon? I was angry with you when we first met and you kept reminding me that 'we are not related.'" She mimicked the smooth baritone of his voice. "But after spending time with you and getting to know the kind, caring, intelligent man you are, I'm so thankful to know you, and I pray that we will be a part of each other's lives for a long time to come."

His dreams were coming true. "So where do we go from here?"

She gave him a puzzled look. "What do you mean?"

"You know—I live in California; you live in North Carolina. How can we make this work when we live so far away from each other?"

"And I don't like California." Larissa scrunched up her nose. "Especially not Los Angeles."

"Well, I think you know why I would have issues with living here."

"No, Solomon, I don't," she said. "Please explain."

"I don't want to get you upset, but I wouldn't feel right living here because of how well-known Pastor David is."

She sighed. "I really wish you'd stop calling him 'Pastor David.' As if all you know of him is his preaching."

"I don't even know that. I wasn't around to hear any of his sermons."

Larissa studied him for a long moment, then reached out and cupped his face in her soft palms. "Are you that dense?" she asked gently. "Don't you know that Uncle David loves you and that he has been hurt by his absence from your life—maybe not as much as you were hurt by his absence, but he was hurt. And now the two of you both have an opportunity to heal. Together."

"I'm still trying to wrap my mind around how I feel about David Davison. Every time I deal with him, I can tell that he's a good man, but then I remember how he treated me, and the two things just don't line up." He paused. "The way Adam did Summer bothers me, too, because it suggests a pattern...like the Davison men have some kind of generational curse or something."

"What are you saying?" Larissa dropped her hands and folded her arms across her chest. "You think that if we get together, you are predestined to cheat on me or something?"

Solomon shook his head vigorously. "Not cheat on you. I can't imagine wanting another woman in my life. But I'm thinking that the Davison curse might have more to do with being destined to disappoint women. And there's something you don't know about me."

"Like what?" She spoke the words so calmly, but Solomon saw the worry creeping into her eyes.

"I'm not a serial killer or anything like that, so relax."

Larissa released a dramatic sigh of relief. "Thank goodness! Boy, you had me scared. I was thinking that I was going to have to act like I was going to the restroom and then sneak out of here."

"See, that's it," Solomon said. "I know that you were just joking, but my biggest fear, now that I've admitted how I'm feeling you, is that you'll just pick up and leave me."

Larissa gave him a look of concern. "Why do you think like that?"

Solomon closed his eyes, trying to shut out the reality of what he'd just said. How many times when he was a kid, after his mother left the house, had he worried that he would never see her again? He'd never been in a relationship longer than six months, always thinking that he needed to break up with his girlfriend before she broke up with him. He probably needed to see a therapist about that, but he couldn't admit his shortcoming to Larissa—not now, when things between them were so new. "I'm thinking about going out on my own so I can practice the kind of law I believe God has designed for me," he said instead.

"Solomon, that's wonderful." Larissa hopped out of her seat and leaned across the table to kiss him. "I'm so proud of you for following your convictions."

Solomon grinned. "I'm excited about it, too. But the thing that worries me is thinking about being in a committed relationship with you while I'm rebuilding my career."

"That's just an excuse, and you know it." Larissa pushed her plate away from her, clearly not interested in her food anymore.

"Why are you getting upset? I just wanted to be honest with you and lay my cards on the table."

"How can you say you're being honest with me when you're not even being honest with yourself?"

Solomon exhaled slowly. "Okay, you're angry. I get it. But let's not say things to each other that we're just going to regret."

Shaking her head, Larissa told him, "I'm not going to regret telling you how much of a jerk you're being right now." She threw her napkin on the table and stood up. "I can't believe that you tell me that you want to be with me one minute, then invent obstacles so that we can't be together the next."

"That's not what I was trying to do." Not this time. At least, he didn't think he was doing that. What was wrong with him? Why had he taken this from a nice romantic conversation to an all-out fight? "Listen to me, Larissa."

"No, you listen to me," she said. She may as well have had smoke streaming from her nostrils. "I think we could be good together, Solomon Harris, and I'm not afraid to say it. I just want you to give us a try. But if that's too much for you, considering your complicated life and all, then you can just call me once you've uncomplicated things." Larissa stormed out of the restaurant without looking back.

Solomon sat at the table for a minute, trying to figure out how he could fix the mess he'd just created. Then he remembered that Larissa was his ride. He left the tip on the table and ran out of the pizzeria.

He reached her car just as she was pulling out of the parking lot. Waving his hands in the air, he yelled, "Come back, Larissa! I rode with you."

She kept driving, and he kept waving until the car was out of sight. When he finally put his hands down and called for a cab, Solomon realized that he had messed things up royally, and he was going to need an intervention to get things right.

An avalanche of tears cascaded down Larissa's face as she pulled out of the parking lot. All her life, she had been so focused on reaching her goals because she wanted to give her aunt and uncle a fruitful return on their investment in her life—love, time, money, resources, and so forth. Getting an education and pursuing a successful career had occupied so much of her life that she'd never made time for love, always figuring that God would send the perfect man for her at the right time.

Now she wondered if God had really sent Solomon, because he was the farthest thing from perfect. Her vision was being severely impaired by the tears. Larissa couldn't stop crying, so she pulled into the shopping center, parked her car, and picked up her cell phone. She hated calling her aunt with her problems—Alma was already dealing with enough problems of her own—but Larissa didn't know where else to turn.

"Funny you should call," Alma said when she picked up the phone. "David and I were just praying for you."

"I—I'm so sorry to bother you, b-but I'm out here at this shopping center, and I'm too worked up to drive my car."

"Larissa, are you crying?"

"Y-yes…"

"Honey, what's wrong? I thought you were with Solomon."

"I was."

"What happened? Why are you so upset?"

"I'm just so angry with Solomon," Larissa blurted out between her tears of emotion and hurt.

"What shopping center?" Alma asked. Larissa told her, and then Alma said, "You're just five minutes away. I'll be right there. Don't go anywhere."

Larissa ended the call, then leaned her head against the steering wheel and continued to cry her eyes out. Before she could even form a cohesive thought, someone was knocking on her window. She looked up.

There was her aunt, standing outside her car wearing her nightgown and robe. Even through her tears, Larissa laughed as she unlocked the door.

"I thought you'd at least take time to change your clothes, Aunt Alma."

"I couldn't," Alma said as she hopped in the car. "I recognized where those tears were coming from, and I knew I needed to be here for you." She reached over and wrapped Larissa in a comforting embrace.

"I had no idea that loving someone could hurt this much," Larissa sobbed into her aunt's shoulder as she admitted what she hadn't even been able to say to Solomon.

Alma pulled some tissues out of the pocket of her robe and handed them to Larissa. "Here, hon. Wipe your face. It's going to be alright."

"How, Auntie?" She sniffed. "How can anything be right when the man I love is trying to find every excuse in the book for why he can't commit to a relationship with me?"

"Don't you worry about that," Aunt Alma said. "We Wilkinson women always get our man. Unfortunately, your mom got the man that her heart desired—a man who led her into all the wrong places and ruined her life. But your dear old aunt also got the man her heart desired. Things didn't go so smoothly at first, but I stuck with him, and my life has been sweeter than I ever thought possible."

"But how did you know it would work out for you?" Larissa asked as she dabbed at her eyes with the tissue.

"I didn't know up here," Alma said, tapping her skull with her fingertip. "I decided to trust God and my heart. I knew that David was a good man and believed that God was big enough to handle everything that concerned us. And you know what?"

"What?"

"God has been faithful, even with all the mistakes that David and I have made."

"So, you think it will be okay between Solomon and me?"

Alma nodded and smiled. "I think it will be more than okay."

CHAPTER 23

Solomon wasn't sure if anything would ever be alright again. With his case finished and Larissa not speaking to him, he decided it was time to pack up and head back home. David had asked that he attend church with the family. David would then drive him to the airport for their last good-bye.

Solomon was asked to sit on the front pew with Alma and David's other children. Adam was out of the hospital, and he and Portia were the first ones seated in the front row, looking as if all was right in their world. But Solomon knew the truth, and he wondered how long they would be able to fake it. Larissa sat down next to Portia. Solomon rushed over, so that Leah or Tamara would not be able to take his spot next to Larissa.

"Good morning," he said as took his seat.

Larissa turned to him, her eyes softening when she saw him. "Good morning," she echoed.

"Do you think we can talk?" Solomon wanted to plead with her to say yes, but he kept his cool and waited for her response. The choir stood up, the organist started playing, and the congregation rose for praise and worship.

Larissa nodded. "After service," she said and then began clapping her hands and singing with the choir.

Solomon threw his hands up and also began to worship God. Larissa was talking to him again. That was truly something to praise God for. A few minutes later, getting in the spirit, Solomon glanced to his right where his half sisters stood. Tamara was clapping her hands and singing praises to God like the rest of them. But Leah looked so sad and withdrawn that he was compelled to reach out and put his arm around her, pulling her close to him.

She hugged him back. "I'm so sorry for how I've treated you, Solomon. I was so wrong."

"I forgive you," he told her. "Stop letting it get you down."

As he released her, she smiled at him and nodded, "I'll try." Then she whispered in his ear so no one could overhear her, "And thanks for being an awesome big brother."

Now Solomon was smiling at her, but it was only a half smile because while he thought it nice that Leah thought of him as her big brother, it wasn't as if they could acknowledge that fact to anyone else. He couldn't even tell Winter that he wasn't just her pretend uncle but her actual uncle. And she could count on him being there for her because they were family.

He glanced around the sanctuary, trying to find Winter. She had come with them to church but had joined up with a few friends as soon as they'd entered the building. He spotted her in the back standing next to Summer. Solomon didn't know how he felt about that. But he knew that Winter loved her mother. He was just thankful that David had arranged for Winter to stay with them during Summer's incarceration, which would start soon. He was also glad that Summer was meeting with a certified counselor several times a week. David was paying for the sessions because he wanted to make sure that Summer got all the help she needed to become the best mother she could be.

While Solomon thought that was a good start, he also felt that Portia, the mother of David's other grandchildren, could use some counseling of her own. There had to be something seriously wrong with any woman who could do what she did, but nobody seemed to be concerned with addressing that.

The choir sat down, and Pastor David stepped up behind the podium. This was his first day back at church since his heart attack, so the congregation went wild, clapping and cheering for him. He looked like a well-rested man rather than a weary man who had gone through heartache, betrayal, and more heartache but still managed to recover and come through it all as vessel even better fit for the Master's service.

David lifted his hands and began lowering them, signaling for the congregation to calm it down and take their seats. He smiled at them as they kept clapping instead. "You all look so beautiful to me," he said. "It feels good to be in the house of the Lord."

Up and down the aisles, all through the sanctuary, people started shouting "Hallelujah!" and "Praise the Lord!" Again David signaled for the congregation to sit. "I really do have something I'd like to talk to you all about today."

One by one, everyone took their seats and sat forward, looking attentive. Pastor David opened his Bible and said, "Please turn with me to Psalm fifty-one." When the pages stopped turning, he began reading, starting with the first verse.

Have mercy upon me, O God, according to thy lovingkindness: according unto the multitude of thy tender mercies blot out my transgressions. Wash me thoroughly from mine iniquity, and cleanse me from my sin. For I acknowledge my transgressions: and my sin is ever before me. Against thee, thee only, have I sinned, and done this evil in thy sight: that thou mightest be justified when thou speakest, and be clear when thou judgest. Behold, I was shapen in iniquity, and in sin did my mother conceive me. Behold, thou desirest truth in the inward parts: and in the hidden part thou shalt make me to know wisdom. Purge me with hyssop, and I shall be clean: wash me, and I shall be whiter than snow. Make me to hear joy and gladness; that the bones which thou hast broken may rejoice.

When he was finished reading, David looked out over the congregation. Tears were running down his face as he said, "For months now, you all have heard false allegations against me, and those of you who love and know me believed us when we told you that what was being said about me wasn't true. I thank you for standing by me.

"But today, I stand before you and confess that I have sinned against my family and against God. For although those allegations were false, my wife and I have hidden another secret for thirty years. It wasn't right for us to do this, and it ends today."

Solomon was holding his breath, hardly able to believe what his ears were hearing. Larissa grabbed his hand and squeezed it.

"You see," David continued, "I am not a perfect man, just a man who happens to love Jesus. But before my wife and I gave our lives to the Lord, I had an affair with another woman, resulting in the birth of a son. My wife and I were separated at the time; but, as I counsel married couples all the time, separation doesn't give you the right to go out and hook up with someone other than your spouse. I learned the hard way that what I did was wrong, and my family has been paying for my infidelity ever since. The biggest price has been paid by my son Solomon, with whom I never had a relationship because I was too ashamed to acknowledge the sinful act I had committed."

David looked down at Solomon and said, "I hope that, one day, you will be able to forgive me for what I did, Son. Because I want to be your father more than anything in this world."

Tears were forming in Solomon's eyes when he realized that David had called him "Son" and, this time, it had felt so right. It felt as if God in heaven was looking down on them and giving them permission to become a family. Solomon stood on shaky legs and strode over to the podium. He put his arms around David and did what he'd wanted to do for so many years…he cried on his father's shoulder. "I forgive you, Dad. I forgive you."

After service, while many of the congregants shook hands with Solomon and welcomed him into the family, several others were upset about the matter. One gray-haired woman stormed up to the front of the church and told Pastor David, "Well, isn't this just terrible. All this time, I thought you were an honorable man, but I'll tell you what. I'm going to be looking for a new church come tomorrow."

"I'm sorry you feel that way, Mother Brown," David gently replied. "But I do understand." He patted her on the shoulder and wished her well. Pastor David had two other conversations like that, but for the most part, his congregation was understanding about this thing that he had done long before giving his life to the Lord.

Portia said to Adam, "I think we can use this. The people are acting all happy now, but if we play our cards right, we can force your father to retire, and you'll be pastor by the end of the year."

Adam turned to his wife. He had loved this woman and had tried to make a life with her, but nothing he did was ever good enough. She would either have to accept him for who he was or divorce him, because he wasn't playing her game anymore. He leaned down and quietly said, "If you even whisper a word against my father, I will make sure the police know that you sent your cousin to rob me."

Portia recoiled as if she'd been slapped. "How dare you!" she hissed. "I didn't send him to rob you. I sent him to get our children's college fund back. You had no right to take that money."

"And you had no right to put me, your husband, in a position to get shot and possibly killed by your maniac cousin."

"I told Ray-Ray not to bring a gun. I never wanted you hurt. How could you even think that I did?"

Adam threw his hands in the air, ready to be done with the whole matter. "I don't know what to think anymore, Portia, but you've got the money back, and now you'll also have to make room for my other child if you want to stay married to me, because I'm not denying Winter's existence anymore." He pointed to David and added, "My father taught me that lesson. I've seen how much pain it causes when you conceal your sins." Adam turned away from her and started for Winter.

Portia grabbed his arm. "I'm warning you, Adam—I'm not like your mother. If you shame me like this, I will divorce you."

Adam pried her hand off his arm finger by finger. "It took me a long time to see it, but you're right, Portia—you are nothing like my mother. Now, if you'll excuse me, I'd like to spend some time with my oldest daughter."

Larissa waited in the sanctuary, waiting on the crowd to die down. Solomon was having the time of his life getting to know the members of the congregation, and she didn't want to rush him. Adam seemed to be having a good time, as well, sitting and talking with Winter several pews over. They were even laughing.

Larissa was proud of her cousin. He had come a long way. But he had a good example to follow. Uncle David certainly hadn't let her down. She was proud to be a part of this family.

As Solomon made his way toward her, Larissa stood and looked at her watch. "You're going to miss your flight if you don't hurry up."

"I'll catch another one," he said with a shrug. "Besides, I need to book a ticket for you." He was grinning in a way that made it impossible for her to know if he was joking.

"Solomon, I told you, I don't want to live in California," she said. "At least, not at this stage in my life."

"Well, how about a visit? I'd like to introduce you to my mother."

CHAPTER 24

Sheila Harris was a beautiful woman, inside and out. Larissa could see why she had caught her uncle's eye. But she thanked God that she hadn't been able to hold him, because the loss of her uncle would have been too much for her aunt to deal with. "It's so nice to meet you. Solomon speaks very highly of you," Larissa told the woman as they shook hands.

Sheila beamed. "He's a good boy. I'm very proud of him."

"Hey, I haven't been a boy since I cut myself shaving. I'm a full-grown man." Solomon then struck a pose like Mr. Universe, flexing his muscles and puffing out his chest.

Larissa and Sheila laughed at him.

"I don't know what's so funny. I worked hard to get these guns." He showed off his arms one more time, receiving another round of giggles for his trouble. He waved them off. "Whatever. I'm still a man."

"Yes you are, Son." Sheila patted him on the back. "A full-grown man," she teased, then laughed again.

"Come on, Mom. You're making me look bad in front of company."

His mother looked around the room as if searching for something. "What company? I know you're not talking about Larissa, because she is not company in my house." She turned to Larissa. "Girl, consider yourself family around here, okay?"

"Yes, ma'am." Larissa was grinning at Solomon, clearly enjoying herself.

Solomon grabbed Larissa's arm. "Come on. I'm taking you sightseeing before she pulls out my kindergarten photos and shames me any further.

Larissa waved her hand. "Oh, I've already seen plenty of embarrassing photos of you. Believe me, the collection that Uncle David keeps isn't all that flattering."

"Hers is worse," Solomon said, nodding toward his mother as he picked up his car keys.

"I'll get your room ready while you're out with Solomon. And don't stop anywhere for dinner, because I'm going to make Solomon's favorite dish."

"Huh. That's the least you can do after embarrassing me."

Larissa and Solomon jumped in his BMW. Solomon turned on the car and backed out of the driveway. "Hmm...where to take you first?" he pondered aloud.

Larissa shrugged. "You don't have to take me anywhere. I was having fun just spending time with your mother."

"The two of you were having too much fun. My ego needs a break from that for a little while. How about we drive over to Warner Brothers Studio and take the tour?"

"Sounds good." And it was. Among the highlights was visiting an actual film set for an up close look at the props, lighting, and special effects.

When the tour was over, they drove down to the Santa Monica Pier and strolled awhile. Not wanting to spoil their appetites for dinner, they grabbed a slice of pizza each and snacked outside, watching the surf, enjoying the feel of the wind whipping across their faces.

"It's beautiful here," Larissa said with a contended sigh. "I can see why you like this place so much."

"You haven't seen anything yet," Solomon said as he guided her to the aquarium. "I love this place because they let you touch the sea creatures."

Larissa smiled as she watched Solomon scurry from one area of the aquarium to the next, putting his hand in the water and playing with the fish and so many other sea creatures that she soon lost count. When Solomon jumped at the chance to help the staff feed the sea stars, Larissa just laughed at him. "You're like a kid playing with toys."

He shrugged. "I used to come here with my mother when I was a kid. She worked two or three jobs at a time, so we rarely had spare time to just hang out. This place was a treat for us. My mom feels the same as I do about it."

"Look at you," Larissa said, grinning at him. "I never pegged you for a mama's boy. But I guess you never know someone until you meet his family."

"Hey, my mom is good people. So, call me a mama's boy if you want. At least she knows my favorite food. I bet you there's vegetarian lasagna with grilled asparagus on the menu tonight."

Larissa furrowed her brow. "I thought you liked meat. I've seen you eat it."

"I do, but I try to eat a balanced diet. My mom is a vegetarian, and she's a wonderful cook, so I know that if she made the dish, it's guaranteed to be good."

Larissa was glad to hear that he watched his diet. She just hoped his standards weren't too high when it came to cooking. "As a doctor, I can totally relate to the desire to eat less meat, but I know I can't cook as well as your mother," she confessed. "Because I've never made the same vegetarian meal twice."

Solomon put his arm around her. "Come on, let's head home. Maybe my mom will let you in on a few of her secrets."

Back at the house, Sheila looked at her son as if he had two heads when he asked her to share her cooking secrets with Larissa. But the moment Solomon left the kitchen, Sheila turned to Larissa with a wink and said, "All I do is add a little garlic and sea salt to my veggies. Onion powder works wonders, too."

Larissa laughed. "Solomon was raving about your vegetarian meals. Can it be that simple? Just add some garlic and salt?"

Sheila opened a cabinet and pulled out a bottle of extra-virgin olive oil. "I use a little of this, too."

Larissa spent the next hour in the kitchen, helping Sheila with the dinner. Solomon sat on a bar stool at the counter, "assisting" by supervising. When his mother arranged the asparagus spears on the baking sheet and began drizzling them with olive oil, Solomon had the nerve to say, "Don't bunch those up. You want to spread them apart a little more so they can breathe." As if he knew so much about cooking. "And don't forget to show Larissa all the goodness you put on the asparagus to make it taste so amazing."

Shaking her head, Larissa picked up the garlic powder and sea salt. "Here's your goodness." She seasoned the spears evenly with a sprinkle of each, then covered the sheet with foil and put it in the oven. "I'm thinking that when we're done with this, I'll sit and watch you make my favorite dish. How does that sound?"

Solomon grinned. "It sounds fine to me, just as long as you don't mind getting your stomach pumped after you eat it."

"He's serious about that," Sheila told her. "I was sick for two days after eating some concoction he came up with. I haven't allowed him into my kitchen since."

Larissa groaned. "Okay, I take it back. I'll fix whatever you want to eat. Just don't cook anything for me. Ever."

Solomon stepped up behind and put his arms around her waist, turning her around to face him. "You've got jokes, huh? Well, I'll tell you what I'm going to do. In the morning when you wake, you'll be smelling all the delicious aromas coming from this kitchen because I'm going to make breakfast for you and Mom."

Larissa sent Sheila a look of mock alarm. "I thought you banned him from your kitchen."

Sheila laughed. "I did, but he's being stubborn because he thinks he has something to prove."

"You don't even know what time we're getting up in the morning," Larissa said to Solomon, knowing full well that he would not be spending the night at his mother's house.

"Oh, I'll get here bright and early, don't you worry. Before you know it, your senses will be assaulted with the wonderful aromas of my home-made breakfast."

⌣⌣⌣⌣⌣

Solomon had let his mouth write a check that his cooking skills could not cash, so after he left his mother's house, he spent the night in his home office scouring the Internet for breakfast recipes. He was going to show Larissa that he was no lightweight when it came to throwing down in the kitchen.

He found a recipe for breakfast tacos and then another for potato-crusted Swiss chard quiche. Both sounded good to him. If he could pull this off, he would be the man. He made a midnight run to the grocery store to purchase all the ingredients, and when he came back home, he stayed up until three in the morning studying the recipes, just as he'd studied during his years of law school. This breakfast was that important to him.

Solomon lay down for a cat nap, setting his alarm for 6 a.m. When he awakened, he quickly dressed and then made his way back to his mother's house. He opened her front door with his key and carried his grocery bags straight to the kitchen, then got busy preparing all the fixings for his quiche. Once he had everything in the pan, he put the quiche in the oven and set the timer, then turned his attention to the breakfast tacos.

By eight in the morning, the kitchen was smelling good, and Larissa and Sheila drifted in to see what he'd created.

"Didn't I tell you that the aroma would wake you?" Solomon bragged, wiping the sweat from his brow.

"You woke us up," Larissa conceded. "Now let's see if you're going to send us to the emergency room."

"Grab a plate and dig in." Solomon handed her a plate and gestured to the smorgasbord of breakfast items.

His mom raised an eyebrow at Larissa. "He cooked all this food; the least we can do is eat it." But the look on her face said that she was anything but sure of her decision.

While she and Larissa filled their plates, he went to sit in the living room. As hungry as he was, his fatigue won out. He just wanted to be awake long enough to gauge their reactions.

Larissa joined Sheila at the kitchen table. When they prayed over their food, the prayer sounded more like a request for God to protect them and safeguard them from any sickness the food might bring.

"Hey," Solomon grumbled from the living room. "I heard that."

Larissa giggled, then tentatively took her first bite of quiche. It was surprisingly delicious.

"Son, this is really good," Sheila murmured. "Thank you for breakfast."

Larissa was about to thank Solomon, too, but when she peeked in the living room, she saw Solomon slumped over on the couch, asleep. She nudged Sheila, who looked over her shoulder.

"If that's not love, I don't know what is," Sheila said as she turned back to her breakfast.

But Larissa couldn't let a comment like that pass without correcting it. "Solomon's not in love with me. He's never said anything like that."

Sheila arched an eyebrow at her. "Honey, I know my son. This is love."

CHAPTER 25

When it was time for Larissa to go back home, Solomon didn't know how he could continue to wake up every morning in Los Angeles when his heart was in Charlotte, North Carolina.

The night before Larissa's early-morning flight, he had a strong urge to talk with someone about how he was feeling. His mom had always been there for him, but he didn't feel right having this conversation with her. He needed a man's perspective, and the only man who came to mind right now was David Davison.

This whole idea of talking to his dad felt strange to him. He'd wanted his dad around for all those years when he was growing up but had no way of getting in touch with him. Now he could reach out and touch him whenever he wanted. Solomon hesitated but then picked up the phone and placed the call.

"Hey, Son," his father answered, albeit groggily. "I was hoping I would hear from you this weekend."

"Were you sleeping?"

"Actually, I just finished my evening prayers."

Solomon glanced at his watch. It was 8 p.m. California time. In his rush to speak with his father, he'd forgotten that the man was three hours ahead. "Dad, I'm sorry to have called you so late. I wasn't even thinking about the time difference."

"I figured you must have something pretty important on your mind. Let's talk."

His dad wasn't rushing him off the phone or acting like there were more important things than him in the world. It felt good to finally have both his parents in his life. "Thanks, Dad. I just don't know what's going on with me these days. I really need a man's perspective on this before I jump into something I'm not ready for."

"Now, if this 'man's perspective' you're seeking has to do with you and Larissa, I hope you know that I'm not going to be the most objective person."

"That's just it—I need you to act as if you don't have a connection to either one of us, so that you can help me figure this out. Okay?"

"Okay, Son, I'll try."

"I'm serious, Dad. I really need your help."

"I'm here for you, Son. Just tell me what's bothering you so we can try to resolve the issue."

Taking a deep breath, Solomon admitted out loud what he had known for a while now: "I'm in love with Larissa."

"You're finally acknowledging it?" David asked. Solomon could hear the smile in his voice.

"I guess I am," Solomon said, rubbing a hand over his face. "She's perfect for me. I love everything about her."

"But…?"

"But, if I'm being honest with myself, I'd have to admit that the only problem standing in our way is me. I'm afraid that I won't be the kind of man she deserves."

"Considering me and Adam, I can see why you would come to a conclusion like that," his father admitted.

Solomon hadn't wanted to come right out and say it, but that was just what had him worried.

"You have to understand," David began, "Alma and I were very young and immature when we got married. So were Adam and Portia, for that matter. We had to grow up in order to realize that we were all each other needed. I don't think you and Larissa will have that problem. You're older and wiser. You know what you want, and with God's help, I doubt that you'll do anything foolish enough to destroy Larissa's love for you."

"You really think she loves me, too?" Solomon felt silly even asking. He sounded like a schoolboy with a crush on the girl next door.

"I think it's time for you and Larissa to sit down and talk."

"I plan to do that tomorrow morning before she gets on the plane."

"Good."

"Just one more question." Solomon wasn't ready to end the call just yet. "Do you think that a man who grew up without a father could become a good father to his own children?"

With a long-suffering sigh, David said, "I wasn't there for you, that is true. But just as Alma and I found the Lord, so did your mother. Not only did I constantly pray for you, but Sheila kept you covered in prayer.

So, even though you didn't have your earthly father, you had your heavenly Father. And He is a better example than I ever could have been.

"As the years go by, and you and Larissa have children, I will be here if you have any questions. But, most important, you will always be able to turn to our Lord and Savior. He will lead and guide you so that you can become the father you need to be."

After talking with his father, Solomon realized that love wasn't something to run away from. He was old enough to know what he wanted, and he was man enough to see it through. The next morning, he picked Larissa up from his mom's house and put her bags in the trunk. But before getting in the car, Solomon pulled Larissa close to him and kissed her, long and full, on the lips. When the kiss was over, he looked into her eyes and finally told her, "I'm in love with you."

Leaning into him, she kissed him again and said, "And I love you right back."

Solomon could see his mother peeking out the door, so he hollered, "Did you hear that, Mom? She said she loves me."

Evidently unashamed at being caught snooping, his mother flung open the door and stepped onto the front stoop. "She's perfect for you. I'm thrilled! Next time you come back to Los Angeles, Larissa, I'll give you all of my recipes."

"Thanks, Ms. Sheila," Larissa said, still in Solomon's arms.

"Come on, let's get you to the airport so you won't miss your flight." Solomon and Larissa jumped in the car and sped down the highway. But the closer they got to the airport, the more he realized that he couldn't let her go without telling her all that was in his heart. So, he pulled off the highway to do just that.

"What's wrong?" Larissa asked as he maneuvered the car into a parking lot. "Why are we stopping?"

Solomon turned off the car, looked up, and realized that he had pulled into the parking lot of a jeweler's boutique. In that moment, he knew that everything his father said had been true. He would not have to worry about a thing, because God would lead and guide him for all the days of his life, even through marriage and fatherhood.

He pointed at the store.

Larissa turned in that direction, looked back at him with a question dancing in her eyes. "Why did we stop here?"

As calmly as possible, he told her, "I'd like to go in that store and pick out a ring for you. But first I need to ask you something."

"Now? In the car?"

"Larissa Wilkinson, I've waited for you all my life, and I don't want to wait another second to know whether you want to marry me as much as I want to marry you."

Tears sprang to her eyes. "Are you kidding? Of course I want to marry you!"

Grinning like a lovesick fool, he said, "Well, come on, then. Let's go pick out a ring before you miss your flight."

Those words halted Larissa. She grabbed hold of Solomon's arm and stopped him from climbing out of the car. "Where are we going to live? I'm in residency in North Carolina, and you have a life out here."

"I just want to pick out the ring today. We'll figure the logistics out before the wedding. But all I care about is that we are together, because wherever you are feels like heaven to me."

"How can I say no to that?" Larissa and Solomon couldn't take their eyes off each other as they walked into the jewelry store arm in arm, united in love.

Coming in Winter 2015

Book Two in the Series

My Soul to Keep

by Vanessa Miller

*G*rowing up, Tamara Davison felt like the princess of her father's ministry empire. She never lacked for anything and thought that life was pretty near perfect. But then, the truth about her father's illegitimate son was revealed, and Tamara stopped being so sure about her fairy-tale life.

Jonathan Hartman has loved Tamara ever since meeting her in college. But Jonathan was raised in a poor town by parents who always struggled to make ends meet. He had to work two jobs while in college, and although he now has a good career with a decent income, he fears that he will not be able to take care of Tamara in the way she is accustomed to being cared for.

When a slick-talking pro-baller tries to sweep his lady love off her feet, Jonathan must find a way to convince Tamara that true love feels so much better than all the money in the world.

ABOUT THE AUTHOR

*V*anessa Miller is a best-selling author, playwright, and motivational speaker. Her stage productions include *Get You Some Business, Don't Turn Your Back on God,* and *Can't You Hear Them Crying.* Vanessa is currently in the process of writing stage productions from her novels in the Rain series.

Vanessa has been writing since she was a young child. When she wasn't writing poetry, short stories, stage plays, and novels, reading great books consumed her free time. However, it wasn't until she committed her life to the Lord in 1994 that she realized all gifts and anointing come from God. She then set out to write redemption stories that glorified God.

Feels like Heaven is book one in Vanessa's third series with Whitaker House. Her previous series are Morrison Family Secrets, comprising *Heirs of Rebellion* and *The Preacher, the Politician, and the Playboy,* and Second Chance at Love, of which the first book, *Yesterday's Promise,* was number one on the Black Christian Book Club national best-sellers list in April 2010. It was followed by *A Love for Tomorrow* and *A Promise of Forever Love.* In addition, Vanessa has published two other series, Forsaken and Rain, as well as a stand-alone title, *Long Time Coming.* Her books have received positive reviews, won Best Christian Fiction Awards, and topped best-sellers lists, including *Essence.* Vanessa is the recipient of numerous awards, including the Best Christian Fiction Mahogany Award 2003 and the Red Rose Award for Excellence in Christian Fiction 2004, and she was nominated for the NAACP Image Award (Christian Fiction) 2004.

Vanessa is a dedicated Christian and devoted mother. She graduated from Capital University in Columbus, Ohio, with a degree in organizational communication. In 2007, Vanessa was ordained by her church as an exhorter. Vanessa believes this was the right position for her because God has called her to exhort readers and to help them rediscover their places with the Lord.